The Bright World of Dandelion Court

The Bright World of Dandelion Court
stories and other lies

Rick Hermann

Free-Range Press
Bellingham, Washington

"The Sons of Porfirio Alonzo" first appeared in the *Kansas Quarterly*, Vol. 8, Nos. 3-4, 1976.

"Progress" first appeared in the *Port Townsend Journal*, Vol. 1, No. 3, 1974.

I gratefully acknowledge Elizabeth Weber for her editorial guidance and her conviction that these stories deserved an audience.

©2011 by Rick Hermann. All rights reserved.
ISBN 978-0-692-01448-6
Library of Congress Control Number: 2011932737
Printed in the United States of America
Free-Range Press
2011

For additional copies, please contact:
Rick Hermann
2214 E. Birch St., Bellingham, WA 98229
360-734-4308   rhermann309@gmail.com

or

Village Books
1200 11th St., Bellingham, WA 98225
360-671-2622   www.villagebooks.com

With love to my wife, teacher, and best friend Lee Willis.
You are my inspiration. Your critiques of these stories were
offered with grace and mercy, and without your encouragement
this book would simply not be.

and

In memory of my sister,
Diane Murray
(1941-2010)

I believe in yesterday.
Paul McCartney

Yesterday's gone.
Chad and Jeremy

Contents

Introduction 1

Say I'm an Indian   (2011) 9

The Sons of Porfirio Alonzo   (1974) 21

The Bright World of Dandelion Court   (2009) 37

Progress   (1972) 55

Mason Dixon   (2010) 71

Forgotten Wife   (2011) 91

Waiting for Zero   (2010) 103

The Moon Shines Tonight   (1971) 115

Like a Father   (1983, 2009) 133

Pure Bob   (2010) 153

silent pictures   (1972) 155

The End of the World,
As Witnessed by David Pickles   (2010) 161

Introduction

My storytelling life began with a creative writing class I took at Washington State University in 1970. Other than the teacher himself, who used a cane to support a bum leg and sported a wry sense of humor and a nicely trimmed mustache, I recall only that I liked the class, and I thought that writing, at least for someone's approval, could be a rewarding activity.

During that semester, I did try to teach myself self-discipline, rising early every morning to write. The results were mixed. I even re-keyed several of John Steinbeck's short stories on my Smith Corona Portable typewriter, giving a tactile dimension to my practice, as though I could absorb the writer's talent by putting his words on paper using my own hand.

In 1972, I carried my typewriter with me to my second attempt at "learning" how to write from someone else when I hitchhiked from Seattle to Port Townsend to attend a writing workshop at the John Woolman School of American Letters, founded by novelist and short story writer Jack Cady. My abilities and perspectives have changed over the years, but I think have learned best of all how to write for myself. Both the art of writing and the business of publishing served me well throughout my editorial career. Recently, however, I have rekindled an old love for the short story format. Fondly recalling a handful of tales I'd written roughly 35 years ago, I included four of them in this collection.

Thus, you have in these pages the perspective of a young man writing his first short fiction, as well as that of a boomer who has with humility and gratitude turned 60.

In fact, I recently attempted to write a story based on my time in Port Townsend, but couldn't get a firm hold on one of the central characters. After several drafts of what I had hoped would be the book's cornerstone story, I decided to try a different approach: I wrote the would-be character's death notice. That took on its own life as the story "Pure Bob," an obituary that becomes a call to celebration.

Some additional comments on the stories found herein:

My intent in "Like a Father" was to write about how art, fiction in particular, can dig more deeply into our souls than we tend to go in our day-to-day lives. In fact, I think I ended up with a fairly accurate piece of psychological autobiography.

I chose for a main character a college student who has a somewhat disturbing obsession with 19th and 20th century German literature. He has a secret-diary type confessional tone to his writing that is highly emotional. The young man has a run-in with his father that separates them profoundly and throws the latter's life into a chaotic, regret-filled period.

When I wrote the first version of this tale in 1983, my father and I were in the process of reconnecting after more than 10 years of silence. I wrote the first version of the story that year. At its center is the estrangement of the son, who is in college, and the father, with whom the son breaks off contact after an essentially trivial matter that triggers a monstrous schism.

Although I lived in Seattle and he in Los Angeles, we got to know one another on new footing, and I enjoyed being with him during visits in Seattle and LA, until he died in 1998. I never showed him the story.

I used to think that the young student was a Germanic exaggeration of myself, a darkly amusing doppelgänger. Now, aside from the fictional touches and bleak conclusion, I'm not so sure it's not just me. Admitting that, even to myself, naturally prompts stark, even fearful conjectures about the character's—my—future. But I have no clear answers to these ultimate questions about my aging and mortality. Nor, do I think, does any of us.

It is disquieting to write so much about what is broken in life—absent fathers, death, ghosts, sexual abuse, insanity. "Waiting for Zero" came to me shortly after I was threatened by two thugs with a six-foot length of chain in broad daylight on a busy street in Bellingham. I managed to talk my way out of what could easily have escalated to physical assault. The emotional residue lingers. This story became my take on random violence, narrated by an unreliable man-boy with more than his share of psychotic impulses. This was the most difficult story for me to write. It haunts me; I'm both attracted to and uneasy with the character of Hank and his suave nihilism.

Many years ago, as I was walking onto the ferry from downtown Seattle to Bainbridge Island and the Kitsap Peninsula, I caught my reflection in a large window: rucksack on my back, beaten-up guitar case in one hand, Smith Corona in the other, wearing jeans, a blue work shirt, and a crumpled, dark-blue, brimmed hiker's hat. There, I thought, is my self-image: the Young Writer and Musician on his way to the aforementioned writing school in Port Townsend.

Not surprisingly, this "character" shows up in "Progress," a story I wrote around that time that takes place in rural western Oregon. The seed for this one came from sketches I'd written of a young itinerant guitar player named Mike and an old fiddler from the hills, Charlie Oliphant, who are in a bar playing Black Mountain Rag, a Doc Watson instrumental. That moment took a few months to percolate, but pieces of story began falling together. What finally made it work was writing from the perspective of Mike's old college friend, who spends the fateful summer in Oregon with Mike and Charlie.

"Progress" was first published in the *Port Townsend Journal*, which has long since disappeared, like the dust blowing across Charlie's land.

Three of these twelve stories are either narrated by or told from the point of view of a juvenile. I don't start out deciding how old the person telling the story should be, but I find that writing from the perspective of youth lends a relative innocence and uncanny way of getting to the meat of the matter that adults often don't possess. My personal favorite young narrator is Jim in "The Sons of Porfirio Alonzo," a story based loosely on a trip I took with my uncle and his son to Baja California one summer. We didn't meet anyone even vaguely resembling Señor Alonzo, but when Jim quits his fruitless surf fishing attempts and just lies down on the warm sand, telling himself that he'd like to stay in Mexico forever, that is me lying there, trying to wish my clunky relatives out of the picture. Señor Alonzo is, of course, another one of my surrogate fathers, like the publishing director Heinemann in "Like a Father."

This story was first published in *The Kansas Quarterly*.

The character of Lee in "The Moon Shines Tonight" was based on my female cousin in Minnesota. In this story, young Ronnie Harlan is driven by his inarticulate fascination with and love for his relative. This story was written to explore the sometimes inexplicable behaviors and emotions that are really just expressions of love. When I wrote the story, I had left the U.S. for a while, catching a flight to Guadalajara, Mexico, where my sister was eking out an ex-pat life. I was totally at sea about my future. I decided that any story that was worth writing and reading had to be about love, in any of love's guises.

My cousin was raised by her grandparents, an ordeal for all involved, but she made the mistake of assuming that her ticket out of the family home was marriage to, not love for, a young man who seemed to truly love her. Her life has been a tragic story, ending with her death on May 23, 2011.

I live on a cul-de-sac that is perhaps more like the insular Dandelion Court of the title story than I care to believe. One day a few years ago, I went for a walk in the woodland park near my home. The worldview of a character named, inexplicably, Old Major Tom Keenan came to me on that walk. I could really sympathize with the guy. He is unhappily divorced, shy and depressed, yet tries hard to understand life and where he fits in the world.

We don't really know Tom's history. Is he disabled? A vet? Between jobs? I tried to build him a past, but ultimately followed the dictum "less is more."

The thing I like most about this story is the affected formality, wryness, and irony in the narrative voice. It emerged as I began writing down loosely related scenes in whatever notebook I had on hand over the course of a few months. When I felt written out, I tore all the Tom Keenan pages from the various notebooks and mounted them on large poster boards. I was then able to visualize the story more clearly.

Note how many times happiness is mentioned in "The Bright World of Dandelion Court," even as Tom struggles with suicidal depression. I didn't intend the juxtaposition; that's just the way it came out.

Just a few blocks away, in the same Dandelion neighborhood, the Partums have lived an uneventful middle-class life. But they're leaving. The opportunity for me to return to Tom Keenan's part of the world, a suburban neighborhood near a large city somewhere vaguely located in the upper Midwest, was irresistible. But in "The End of the World, As Witnessed by David Pickles," the Partums become part of another family's life outside the Dandelion neighborhood, in a story about delusional thinking, memory loss, fragmented families, the alienation of what's left of the middle class, and insanity.

Since I take the same medications for Parkinson's disease that David Pickles is prescribed, I am aware of their potentially serious cognitive side effects. I have found that the cruelest joke about psychotic, schizophrenic, or delusional episodes is that while you are in those states, you don't realize you are insane.

I wrote "silent pictures" when I was reading French author and film director Alain Robbe-Grillet, who in his writing challenges his readers to piece together the story and its emotional significance. Many years after writing this piece, I came across Susan Sontag's story, "Project for a Trip to China," which I admire and which bears stylistic similarities to "silent pictures." In retrospect, it seems as if I took Robbe-Grillet and Sontag to Minnesota and mixed them all together with the waters of the Big Muddy. But I don't presume to view "silent pictures" as either a poor man's Robbe-Grillet or a paean to Sontag. In a cluelessly workman-like way, I wrote a few lines each day, until it seemed done. I believe that at one time this may have been called experimental fiction.

"Mason Dixon" started with the notion of a baby shot so fast from her mother's womb on the birthing bed that no one could grab hold of her. That baby became 10-year old Shush, the main narrator of the story. I had lots to work with here. My wife and I had lived in the South in the mid-1980s. I decided at some point that I could not tell the story without additional perspectives—hence, each narrator's part is called out. Shush's mom Valerie has multiple sclerosis of the remitting/relapsing kind; Shush just calls it "em-ess." Her Aunt Debbie is barely able to hold her life together. Shush's dad Richard is an ambiguous, almost sympathetic character, in denial about his wife's disease, hiding inside of his work. Frustration drives him into an affair with a woman at his office.

My wife and I go to a rustic resort on eastern Vancouver Island every fall to celebrate our anniversary. There is a particular spot on the rocky shoreline where I sat last September with notebook and pen. All of a sudden, I was writing words that seemed to come from outside of me.

That kind of mystery is powerful. After I had written the first paragraph of "Forgotten Wife," I knew something was up, especially with the scrubber made of one hundred porcupine quills, which had over time scrubbed a hole through a cast-iron cooking pot. Things soon became even weirder, and I just went where the characters took me. It came out basically in one draft.

I have no Native American ancestors that I am aware of. I recall an Indian elder and professor who taught at Western Washington University once saying to a discussion group at a human-rights film festival, "A lot of white people want to become Indians. If you know someone like that, tell them we already have enough."

My younger adopted brother is First Nations, from the Upper Nicola Band, a member tribe of the Okanogan Nation. The Upper Nicola preserve is in B.C. near Merritt. My mother and stepfather adopted him when he was four, and he had a very rough time finding his identity in his late teens and early 20s. It took him years to discover his Indian heritage and what was left of his family, and to integrate that into his experience growing up in a racist society.

"Say I'm an Indian" is the most recent of my stories. I don't think racism is a theme, but I write from the white perspective and don't pretend to understand what it's like not to be white.

I really like the characters in this story, especially Gary Ajeo, a middle-aged restaurant owner with a multicultural heritage. He cooks tapas in Bow, Washington, and feeds writers on tour because cooking is his passion. In Gary I see something of my brother: a combination of easefulness and pride.

The main characters in the story are Priscilla Doinke and romance novelist Jack Steinbeck. Doinke is Steinbeck's public relations coordinator and driver on a puddle-jumping, book-signing tour up the West Coast to promote Steinbeck's latest tome. Doing reconnaissance, Doinke visits Forks and Roslyn, Washington-state towns used as locations for recent television shows and movies. "Everywhere is always somewhere else," she muses.

I've never been on a book tour, so the narrative details are guesswork on my part. I also have yet to decide whether I agree with PR flack Doinke when she voices her underlying suspicion that "fiction is just a temporary alliance of lies."

Say I'm an Indian

Steinbeck's West-Coast tour to launch his new novel, *East of Elko, Nevada*, continued into its third week, and on this particular evening the writer was in the back seat of a new black Prius waiting for his publicist to clear a path to the podium. She had told Steinbeck that it was an independent bookstore, to which Steinbeck growled in his emphysemic voice, "Independent of what?"

Steinbeck did not see many cars parked nearby, which made him nervous. It was already winter dark at four in the afternoon. Cold as hell, too.

Independent, Steinbeck well knew, meant being on the endangered species list in the world of bookselling, and woe be to the Luddite pen and ink writers like him who still didn't know how to tweet and didn't want to know. Steinbeck was old school. He still thought of a book as words printed in ink on sheets on paper. Steinbeck also knew he was doomed not by any lack of talent, but by his stone-age level of media savvy. He hadn't a clue what could be worth reading on a "blog," certainly not all that stream-of-consciousness drivel. Not surprisingly, Steinbeck had grown bitter, watching success pass him by, propped up for a time by his eager young publicist Priscilla Doinke, who wrote a successful blog called Zombie Jesus. Steinbeck didn't relate to the nihilism. But he put her sacrilege aside and generally did as Priscilla told him to do.

East of Elko, Nevada, Steinbeck's most ambitious effort to date, centered on the trials and tribulations of the Lane family, including a King Lear-like father and three infighting daughters, as they all struggled to maintain the family's primacy in the sheep-ranching business of northeastern Nevada, and their conflicting desires to control the business. There was a lot of sex along the way, which stopped short of depicting any instances of bestiality, although human-sheep perversions were alluded to. Steinbeck did not want to shock or alienate his primary audience: women between 35 and 65 years of age.

Reno, Sacramento, Bend, Eugene, Sand Point, Coeur d'Alene, Tacoma, Seattle, and now Bow. He was almost done with the western puddle jump, and it couldn't end fast enough to suit him.

The venue Steinbeck waited to enter tonight was the Fire

Hearth Reading and Tapas Bar, located in the very small town of Bow, Washington, on a sharp turn in the Farm-to-Market Road that slowed traffic in and through town. It was not far from Chuckanut Drive, which wound its scenic way along the water to the southern reaches of Bellingham. The population of Bow was around 250, a half-hour drive to Mt. Vernon or Bellingham. Seattle, from which they'd set out earlier in the afternoon, was 75 miles south. Ms. Doinke hadn't been able to book a read-and-sign at Elliot Bay Books, which was in the process of moving to Capitol Hill and wasn't scheduling events. Doinke knew, however, that Elliot Bay had coordinated events elsewhere for Kurt Cobain biographer Charles Cross and for *Cold Mountain* author Charles Frazier. Priscilla didn't share this knowledge with Steinbeck.

As Steinbeck waited outside in the car, he tried not to think of anything, which was easy. This was the good part of doing the circuit, if there was anything good about any of this nonsense. He didn't have to face the typewriter every goddamn morning. Every day on the road had a new rhythm depending largely on the activities of the previous night. He liked that, but was disappointed in the lack of even modest numbers of readers and potential book-buyers at his readings and signings. In Seattle, at the much-smaller Cove Books, an eclectic shop that had some first editions and other rare books, 12 people sat in folding chairs while Steinbeck read from *East of Elko, Nevada*. Only two bought books for him to sign.

  Steinbeck's publicist and traveling companion, Ms. Doinke, from the small Oakland subsidiary of a New York publishing house, a young woman of German descent with dark hair and fine Aryan features (or Steinbeck so perceived), was at the moment inside the almost empty restaurant and bookstore in Bow with the owner, Gary Ajeo. They were trying to figure out why no one had shown up. Gary just shrugged.

  "It was on the calendar." He thought about it. "Let me call Jimmy Cole over at Swinomish and see what the tribe is doing tonight. Usually everyone's at the high school basketball game on Wednesday night."

  When he called Jimmy, that's when Ajeo first heard about the miracle that had occurred just hours earlier at a quarantined ICU bed at Children's Hospital. The phone was set on speaker because Gary had trouble hearing non-amplified phone calls, so Doinke heard the whole thing.

As Jimmy, who was Tommy Jefferson's uncle, told the tale, his Lummi nephew—the son of well-known and highly regarded parents in the tribe who had died in a car accident two years back—had been playing in a basketball game inside the covered blacktop courts up in the reservation town of Marietta. Tommy was nine years old. Late in the game, he drove for a lay-in during a U-10 game, was pushed from behind, went down hard, and split his lip as he collided with the asphalt.

There was some blood, but the boy seemed to take it in stride. Someone took him to the tribal nurse out on Haxton Way, and she finessed a butterfly dressing to staunch the bleeding and avoid the need for stitching. This had happened a week ago. The day after the accident, Tommy's temperature skyrocketed to 103 F° and the flesh around his wound started to fester, blistering his skin. Jimmy Cole, who was Tommy's legal guardian, got him into the Dodge Grand Caravan and drove the boy 95 miles to Children's Hospital in Seattle. By then, the affected area had grown.

"You're gonna be fine," Jimmy told the boy, who now seemed unconscious as they wheeled him into a quarantine area. He heard the emergency doc say *necrotizing fasciitis* as the door clicked shut. Jimmy had never heard of it. He was terrified of losing Tommy, the favorite nephew he'd promised to take good care of and bring up right.

Gary Ajeo, who vaguely knew Tommy Jefferson, was anxious to cut to the chase, but there was no hurrying Jimmy Cole, who stood like a sentinel guarding the realm of time from those who tried to steal it, make up for it, cram useless activity into it, or save it.

"Ladies came out from the Lummi Nation Baptist Church and drove down to Seattle to pray for Tommy. By now most of his face was affected, Tommy was being pumped full of antibiotics, and surgeons were removing skin from his face; it was awful. But those ladies sat in the waiting room and they prayed all through one night and the next, and then the miracle happened."

"What was the miracle?" Gary asked.

"The infection stopped spreading. In fact, it just disappeared. 'Course, Tommy's face'll need to be reconstructed with skin grafts, which could take years, but he's okay. The surgeon was mystified—said he'd never seen spontaneous healing like this in a case spreading aggressive like that. Elma Jack, who was prayin', is going to get the Church to certify Tommy's recovery as a miracle. They had prayed for God's holy intercession on Tommy's behalf, and, by God, God listened."

Priscilla Doinke knew something about the taxonomy of miracles and decided not to mention that the Church, at least the Catholic Church, was extremely cautious about accepting the validity of putative miracles. It maintained particularly stringent requirements in validating the miracle's authenticity, using its Inquisition-like purview and the power wielded by the Congregation for the Causes of Miracles, the members of which played the devil's advocate, in a manner of speaking, trying to find any loophole in claims for miraculous events. Miracles were not inexpensive for the Catholic Church to sanction or maintain.

Jimmy Cole, coming back to Gary's question about basketball, finally said, "Yeah, everyone's up at Lummi watching the Black Hawks try to get past the Braves. You oughta come up."

Steinbeck, still in the car, by now seething with impatience and feeling disregarded, started honking the horn outside. Priscilla rolled her eyes.

"That's Jack's subtle signal that he's ready to do whatever it is he needs to do," she said. "I've got to tell him something about the reading."

"We could drive up to Lummi," Gary suggested. "Just tell Jack that we mixed up the schedule," he added, smiling.

"One thing," Priscilla began carefully. "Mr. Steinbeck, doesn't relate all that well to . . . indigenous people. . . "

"Just say Indians," Ajeo interrupted.

"Excuse me?"

"Okay," Gary began, taking a sip of water from his bottle of glacial melt. "My ancestry is Japanese-Mexican, Upper Nicola, from the Jack family, and Lummi. On my mother's side, there was a lot of problems with alcohol on the rez up there in B.C. My mom sent me out for adoption when I was like three, through the agency in Spokane, and I lived with a white family for the next 19 years. It took me another five years to put together a picture of who I am. My uncle Jefferson Solomon is the president of the Lummi Nation board of economic development. My mother and dad drank themselves to death on the reservation near Merritt. I drank since I was in junior high. I don't touch it now. So don't say I'm *indigenous*, to be polite or politically correct or something." Ajeo put his clenched fist against his heart. "I'm Indian. Just say Indian."

As part of her reconnaissance in the Pacific Northwest weeks prior to the tour with Steinbeck, Ms. Doinke took some personal time to drive to the town of Forks, Washington, where the hot commodity was vampire paraphernalia created during the popularity of the Twilight series of novels and then movies; and Roslyn, the town just east of Snoqualmie Pass, which had been depicted as the Alaskan town of Cicely in the TV show "Northern Exposure." In movies and on TV, she thought, everywhere is actually somewhere else. She tucked this thought away.

"Fiction is just a temporary alliance of lies," she once said to Steinbeck. "Everything is believable, and nothing is true." Priscilla Doinke usually didn't get discouraged, but she was working on her own novel, on top of her Zombie Jesus blog. Right now, her novel was stalled. Just the thought of writing without making a fool of herself made her sick to her stomach.

Doinke's pre-tour assignment was really to check out the Indian casinos that attracted a lot of people to their stage shows. North of Seattle, there was a casino just about every ten miles along the I-5 corridor. Muckleshoot, Skykomish, Tulalip, Swinomish, Skagit, Lummi, Nooksack. She envisioned Steinbeck and other authors in her stable on tour doing performance readings in casino lounges, and laughed at the preposterousness of what had seemed like a good idea back in the office.

Just at the top of the hill referred to as Bow Mountain, a couple miles east of Bow, Priscilla Doinke had stopped at the casino owned by the Upper Skagit Indian tribe. It was close to I-5, and lit up at night like a nuclear accident. The manager, a polite man named George Blades, genially told Ms. Doinke that although he had heard of him, Mr. Steinbrook was, to be honest, a second-rate magician. Blades's entertainment team was committed to offering the public a quality show, he said. "Do you represent any Elvis impersonators?"

Doinke was actually relieved that she was being given the brush-off. Marketing sent me out on this *assignment* and they're laughing at this right now, she thought.

"We're sorry," said Mr. Blades, smiling sympathetically, "but we need relevance. Your guy, Steinbrook, means nothing to our target demographic. Is that a Jewish name?"

Working with Steinbeck was an experience that ranged from difficult to impossible. Steinbeck found it easy to become "Steinbeck" at the drop of a compliment, a favorable review, or an advance on his next book. It had been his idea, not Marketing's, to arrange book readings and signings at casinos.

His only Indian friend (Christ, the only redskin he'd ever even talked to, when they met at a rehab clinic in L.A.) was Ron Jack, a part Colville, part Lakota Sioux native American First Nations aboriginal pre-Columbian indigenous individual who referred to himself as an Indian. Ron encouraged him. "Ind'ns like stories," Ron Jack said, waving a hand.

And so it was that Priscilla Doinke tried to book a tribal casino lounge for a read-and-sign, but got nowhere. She then tried the schools, and heard back only from the director of the Lummi Nation Head-Start program, who assumed that Steinbeck wrote books for children.

Steinbeck, possessed of a desire for admiration and understanding that could be not easily be satisfied, especially by those closest to him, angrily told Doinke he would not read to children.

Nor would children likely want to be read to by a beastly, scowling white man with hair growing out of his ears. Steinbeck's novels and stories, hardly children's books, were suffused with a kind of Elizabethan melancholy, with dreary asides leading the reader through a labyrinth of sadness—dark corridors spreading in all directions, none of them the right path. Along the way, sexual encounters of all description were consummated in the shadows. Steinbeck's research formula was one part history, three parts women's magazines and romance novels, and the rest he made up, as one would expect a novelist to do.

Priscilla Doinke opened the driver's door and slid in behind the wheel, looking at Steinbeck though the rear view mirror.

"Wrong publicity, Jack. No reading scheduled here tonight," she lied. "My bad." She used that pouting, "Please forgive me even though I don't give a shit whether or not you do" look. Doinke may have been more of a pain in the ass than an asset as far as Steinbeck was concerned, but she had a young publicist's verve and pluck, eager to make good of a bad situation. To *his* credit, in Doinke's estimation, Steinbeck had never hit on her. He seemed somewhat emasculated by his present physical condition.

"What the hell were you doing in there?" Steinbeck demanded. "Reading *Valley of the Super-Bloggers?*" This was Jack's favorite tease, and it so annoyed Priscilla that she threatened to put it on her web site in her Top Ten Stupidest Comments list.

"So," Steinbeck, pleased with his dig, asked, "what do we do now?"

"Do you like high school basketball?" she asked.

"No, I do not," Steinbeck answered, although he wasn't really sure if he did or if he didn't.

"That's what we're going to do," said Doinke, as she pushed the *Start* button on the Prius dashboard. What a concept, she couldn't help thinking every time she engaged the ignition. A button to start the car that says Start. "Gary's taking us to see a game."

Steinbeck merely sighed, then settled back in his seat like the prisoner he made himself out to be. The prisoner had just learned the length of his jail term, and was weighing the potential costs and benefits of squawking too loudly about it.

Steinbeck was in a bad mood, due partially to seasonal affective disorder, partially to situational anxiety and the pain in his ankle and the lack of any Percocet, and partially to untreated chronic depression. There wasn't really much room left in there for anything else, except that now he was hungry, too.

How delicately he balanced on the thin ridge between the reality of his dependence on Priscilla Doinke and his tendency to indulge in thinking the darkest thoughts possible, which conveniently distanced him from everyone around him.

When Gary Ajeo got into the front seat and introduced himself, Steinbeck merrily growled, "Ajeo. Is that lah-teen-o?" Priscilla groaned audibly. Ajeo just smiled.

"Not exactly," Gary said in a genial manner. "My ancestry is Mexican, Japanese, and Lummi Indian. Some other things too. Priscilla just heard my spiel about who I come from. I've just kinda wrapped all the ethnic stuff up into who I am: a guy who likes to read books and prepare different kinds of food. Food's my revolution."

At his restaurant, tapas were popular. Ajeo also prepared native foods, including local seaweed and fiddle-head fern buds with eulachon oil and locally caught salmon. He was popular among the locals as well as those who had read about Gary Ajeo in *Sunset* or the now defunct *Gourmet* and came from as far away as Idaho to sample his fare. Gary tried to stay below the radar as much as possible. "I don't like the light shining on me the way some people do," Gary said.

It was true that Gary loved to read. One thing he found true about book authors is that they liked to eat. So it was easy to lure them to stop over in Bow for dinner in exchange for a reading and signing hour. There was a local population of people who had been to college, and had careers, and finally showed up in this corner of the Skagit delta and ended up staying. It was generally an easy matter to fill the place for a reading.

Tonight was different. He'd just taken Doinke's word for it that Jack Steinbeck would be a crowd pleaser. And nothing else much was happening anywhere near the small town on the Skagit delta tidelands at the base of the Chuckanut Mountains on a Wednesday night in January.

Except Indian hoops up north.

This week, the LaConner Braves, including kids from the Swinomish reservation, were up at Lummi playing the Black Hawks, the best, scariest Indian basketball team in the Pacific Northwest.

Steinbeck's ankle hurt like a son-of-a-bitch as Priscilla Doinke sped up I-5 to Slater Road, headed west, then turned south at the Lummi Casino toward the high school. Still healing from an injury sustained in a fall while he was taking the garbage out, the ankle kept Steinbeck confined to a wheelchair borrowed from the Lion's Club in Boise. Folded up, it barely fit into the back of the Prius.

The Lummi High School parking lot was filled, with cars parked along the road as far as he could see. Fortunately, they found a handicapped spot near the gym and pulled in. Not having spoken a word for the whole hour it took to get to Lummi from Bow, Steinbeck now looked despairingly at the ratty-looking gymnasium and asked, "Is this it?" Priscilla opened the hatchback and unfolded the wheelchair, clamping on the leg braces that struck out in front like a cattle catcher on an old steam locomotive. Steinbeck grunted as he transferred to the wheelchair, which he loathed.

"It's not much from the outside," said Gary, "but inside, different story. One hundred percent Indian pride. I took McPhee to a game here once. He loved it, wanted to do a book about Indian hoops."

"John McPhee?" Steinbeck croaked. "You know him?"

"Nah, not really," Gary said as Priscilla pushed Steinbeck's wheelchair up the sidewalk towards the gym. "But he likes to come to Bow—he visited like four or five times after he wrote *Coming into the Country*. He was just wandering around the Skagit Valley in this old Plymouth. I'd just bought the business and was cooking some weird food. He ate it. Nice guy."

Steinbeck crumpled a little lower in the wheelchair. Ajeo bought tickets, and then Steinbeck was in the gym. The stands were packed, and an overflow crowd comprising a couple hundred parents, high school students, community college basketball scouts, Indian kids, and local basketball fans looking for a great game stood against the walls and covered every inch of space behind the out-of-bounds lines. Steinbeck heard an incredible roar—something had happened, somebody had scored—but he couldn't see anything.

Doinke had forgotten him, even though she still held the handles of the wheelchair, and he heard her begin cheering behind him. Ajeo was craning his neck, trying to get a view of the court.

Steinbeck began to feel claustrophobic. The heat from all the bodies inside the gym, the lights glaring in his eyes, the unmuffled roars from the crowd, the slap of sneakers on the hardwood floor, the voices of the players screaming out warnings and encouragement to hustle and crash the boards on defense, all made Steinbeck feel nauseated and trapped.

The memory of playing a game with his older brother Kurt—actually it was more a form of sibling abuse than a game—came up with horrifying clarity, so that for a moment Steinbeck was no longer in the stiflingly hot gym but in a world that had been gone for more than 50 years.

When they were kids, Kurt forced Jack to lie down on the bed, then walked back to the door and re-entered the room like Boris Karloff playing Frankenstein. As Steinbeck lay helpless on the bed, his brother bent over him and tickled Jack in the ribs and under his arms until Jack was almost unable to breathe. Jack hated it. The only way to escape from this torture was to say "I'm an Indian." Then Jack was released. But if he tried to escape too quickly, Kurt would push him back down and start tickling again until Jack gasped, "I'm a squaw!" The last time this happened, Jack was eleven, Kurt thirteen. Jack, getting taller, now matched Kurt's strength. Nonetheless, one day Kurt pushed him down, but when he began trying to tickle, Jack fought back. Kurt turned red-faced with rage and yelled "Say I'm an Indian, goddamn it!" Jack pushed hard against Kurt's chest, so hard that Kurt fell over backwards, landing on his butt, dazed. Jack felt power surging through his body, but also sensed the terror returning. Would Kurt try to kill him?

Then Kurt started to laugh, and pretty soon Jack started laughing too, and they whooped and yelled like Sioux Indian braves returning home after the Battle at Little Bighorn.

That was the last time they ever played "Say I'm an Indian."

Steinbeck was brought back to his senses by a change in the quality and volume of the roaring that surrounded him. The crowd quieted a little, but the pep band heated up with a horn-heavy rendition of "Gimme Some Lovin'."

"Priscilla, I can't see a goddamn thing!" Steinbeck growled over his shoulder. "What the hell am I doing here if I can't see anything?"

"Sorry, Jack. The third quarter's over. Nobody's budging, but I'll wheel you through so we can find a place." Priscilla actually steered Jack out onto the court, looking for a chink in the solid wall of fans. From this vantage, Steinbeck could read the scoreboard on the wall behind one of the baskets:

Home - 54

Visitor - 55

Three of the four quarter bulbs glared red. A buzzer sounded and somebody yelled, "Get off the court!" The pep band stopped playing as the roar of cheering increased again to hearing-impairment levels as the two teams walked onto the court. A space opened in the corner opposite the gym entrance and Priscilla pushed Jack's wheelchair that way, turned it around and backed it into the out-of-bounds area so that Jack had an unimpeded view of the whole court. The man standing beside him said to Priscilla, "Pretty good game tonight." He seemed relaxed and peaceful about whatever outcome might follow. They'd lost Gary Ajeo back in the third quarter.

Steinbeck felt like he needed to be for one team or the other if he was to survive the next fifteen minutes of tedium. He decided on "Home," because he thought of himself as a person who could come from behind to win. Every book he wrote tried to battle him to a stalemate, and yet he usually won the war.

Although not solid on the specific rules of basketball, Steinbeck could now at least follow the flow of the game. As the teams tore back and forth on the court, passing, setting picks, battling for position under the basket, and finally either shooting or losing the ball out of bounds to the opposing team, or having it stolen by a pickpocket defending guard, Steinbeck understood that the way these kids played was like hand-to-hand combat.

"Doinke," he said, leaning back—the use of Priscilla's last name generally meant that Steinbeck was in a rare good mood—"this is incredible. The aggressiveness, just amazing."

The lead changed hands continuously until the Lummi team went on a tear during the final two minutes and buried the LaConner Braves with smothering defensive pressure and by moving the ball inside to their big man, who scored and drew fouls. The defense collapsed in on him, but it didn't make any difference. The tall guy was possessed; everyone, even Steinbeck, could see the guy so in the zone that it was scary. On a steal and a fast break with seconds left in the game, the big man trailed in for a soft pass which he slammed down in a dunk, putting an exclamation point on the victory.

Mayhem ruled as the Lummi fans flooded the court, hoisting team members on strong shoulders to celebrate their win. Steinbeck thought that he didn't feel like a claustrophobic outsider anymore. He was part of something bigger; he recognized an element of his life that had always been missing, and which he now found in the unlikeliest of places. In the dark of winter, on a night that didn't go his measly, narrow way. He felt, for the first time in years, that there was another way to live his life, although he had no idea what that meant. Maybe, just as he'd chosen to be a writer, he could also choose not to be a writer. Being only a second-rate writer especially made the prospect of doing something else seem attractive.

Steinbeck considered this revelation to be a miracle. He wanted to stand up and cheer, but his ankle still hurt like a son-of-a-bitch. As he and Priscilla Doinke waited for the crowd to get smaller as fans slowly left the gym, Jack Steinbeck tried not to feel anything, because he was afraid if he did, what he felt would be so raw and overpowering that his heart would break.

The Sons of Porfirio Alonzo

Señor Alonzo was fat, too, maybe even a little fatter than Uncle Ray, but he seemed to carry it with much more dignity. Ray had fat, fleshy jowls and flabby legs. Señor Alonzo's weight was concentrated above his belt and below his collar and it always looked pretty solid under his clothes. When he made a big smile, which was just about the only kind of smile Señor Alonzo knew, there was this odd sort of movement to his midsection that always startled me when I saw it. It's almost impossible to explain from memory. The best I can say is that it was a kind of quivering, as though his smile alone couldn't contain the joy he felt and it was necessary for other parts of his body to help express it. You might say that his belly smiled. I could look at it without seeing his face and tell whether or not Señor Alonzo was cheerful.

The first time we saw him, he was not cheerful. He had a flat tire on the road between Tijuana and Ensenada and he was pretty upset about it. We saw him standing by the side of the road when we were still a good distance away, and I thought that Uncle Ray was going to ignore him, but when he saw us coming, Señor Alonzo stepped out in the middle of the road and began waving his arms over his head. Uncle Ray cursed these damn Mexicans and started pumping the brakes. We had a lot of weight to bring to a stop, what with the twenty-foot trailer behind the camper. The Mexican stepped up to Uncle Ray's window.

"No hablo Español," Uncle Ray let him know right off.

"I have a goddamn flat tire," the Mexican said, "and no spare. My spare's at home in the garage."

"Oh," Uncle Ray said weakly. He looked a little disappointed. "Oh, then I guess we could take a look."

It was really a useless gesture, looking at the thing, but I guess it was the least we could do. The tire was ripped up pretty badly.

"It doesn't look too good," Tom offered. Tom was Uncle Ray's boy. He was big and fleshy too.

"I don't think we can help you," Uncle Ray told the Mexican. He took pains to speak very clear, precise English. He also spoke louder than necessary, as if by raising his voice the meanings of the words would somehow become more clear. "It's a very bad blow-out," he said shaking his head sadly. "Very bad." He was practically yelling, which didn't help matters.

"Maybe we could give him a lift into Ensenada, Uncle Ray," I suggested.

I'm sure that Uncle Ray was not pleased with my suggestion. He hemmed and hawed and looked at the tire and shook his head even more sorrowfully than before.

I'm also convinced that it was this same suggestion which caused Señor Alonzo always to be nice to me during the times after that day when we happened to meet. When I made it, he had smiled hugely. That was the first time I saw his belly smile. It was a very warm feeling he gave me, and I was glad I'd spoken.
"I'm not certain we should do that, Jimmy," he said to me.

"I live in Ensenada, you know," the Mexican had said to Uncle Ray. "I could pay you for a lift."

Uncle Ray was a man who did not particularly care to get mixed up in other people's affairs, but once he could see no way out, a deep-seated love for his fellow man obliterated all manifestations of selfishness.

"Oh, come on," he said. "We'll take you in for free." Uncle Ray was really a swell person down deep. We all hopped into the cab. It was cramped with four of us, so I got elected to ride in the camper. I could see into the cab, but I couldn't hear. All I remember is the Mexican, who sat in the middle, turning from side to side flailing his huge hands about like an enthusiastic tour guide while Uncle Ray hunched over the steering wheel and looked miserable. Ray didn't think much of people who talked a lot.

I remember, as we drove into Ensenada, that it seemed like the second dirtiest town I'd ever visited. Tijuana was the dirtiest. It shocked me to see people eating food bought from the little wooden carts that the vendors, old men for the most part, pushed up and down the dusty streets amid swarms of shiny fruit flies. I was glad that we'd brought plenty of food from home.

Uncle Ray pulled up in front of a store that reminded me of an A&P, tinted windows and a cool look inside, and up in the cab I saw the Mexican pointing excitedly past Uncle Ray's nose toward the windows plastered with slash-prices and bargains painted blue and red on white butcher paper, just like in the States. That store was his. You could just tell. Uncle Ray, though, didn't seem real interested and when he nodded his head impatiently at the Mexican's gestures—you know, the way you nod when you want to humor someone—I thought Jesus, Uncle Ray, you might think it was pretty good too if you owned a supermarket.

When the Mexican got out of the cab, he thanked Uncle Ray and took out his wallet, about to offer some money. But Uncle Ray waved the Mexican's offer aside.

"Forget it," he said.

The Mexican came back to the side window of the camper and waved and smiled at me.

"So long, *muchacho*!" he said. He half-turned and gestured toward the store again as if to say, "Nice, isn't it?" and I thought, yeah, it really sort of was, and nodded my head to try and make up for Uncle Ray, who was rudely gunning the engine. "Porfirio Alonzo," the Mexican said, still pointing. I could hardly hear him above the rising crescendo of Ray's V-8. "That's me."

Sure, there was his name right over the electric-eye doors. That's what he was pointing at. I nodded even more vigorously and waved.

We were on a fishing trip, and Uncle Ray had heard about this great place from some of his pals at the auto shop. It was called Playa del Cabrillo and it was just south of Ensenada. His pals had said that anybody going to Baja California hardly ever went farther than Ensenada and so Playa del Cabrillo would most likely be deserted, except maybe for a few Mexican fishermen.

When we finally found it, we had to wait for four hours until another family that was leaving moved their trailer and there was space for us in the trailer park. Uncle Ray paid some money to a sharp-looking American man in a pin-striped sport shirt and we parked and hooked up the electricity to the trailer. We hadn't seen the beach yet, but the man in the sport shirt said that it wasn't very far away. I could smell the sea.

Tom and I wandered around, and right in the middle of the trailer park we found a keen recreation hall with more pinball machines and pool tables than I'd ever seen before. The American man smiled at us as we went in and asked us how we liked Mexico.

"It's got a real nice flavor to it," Tom said. I think I rolled my eyes a little bit because it sounded like he was talking about ice cream instead of geography. The man just smiled and told us to go on inside the rec hall and take a look if we wanted.

"Can kids play pool here?" Tom asked.

"Sure, you bet," the man said.

Tom's eyes narrowed some. He gave me a sly sort of glance and winked. "See you later on tonight," he said to the man in the sport shirt.

Playa del Cabrillo was part of a large, crescent-shaped bay that must have been ten miles wide at the mouth. Waves feathered white and broke over a reef guarding the entrance. Around noon the three of us, me and Tom and Uncle Ray, walked with our poles out along the beach to the point where the reef joined dry land, because, according to Uncle Ray, that's where the fish were. On the way, we ran into this old Mexican man who was selling dead minnows for bait. He was sitting in a little wind-swept cabaña looking out at the sea, and he told us that dead minnows were the only thing that would catch these fish. Uncle Ray bought a milk carton full.

I'd never fished in the surf before, and when I cast my bait out, the waves would wash it right back into shore. After three or four casts I laid my pole down on the sand, took off all my clothes except my shorts, and waded out to try and catch some of the smaller waves in the shorebreak. The water was cold, but it felt good and refreshing. It made me want to stay in Mexico forever.

Our plan had been to go out on one of the half-day boats the next morning, and so we had to drive back into Ensenada that afternoon and buy tickets. Most of the fishing boat offices in Ensenada are scattered along the first street up from the waterfront, and we drove up and then back, up and then back, two or three times along that same stretch, looking for a respectable outfit. Uncle Ray slowed down in front of each place and peered suspiciously in through the doors and windows. Several dark faces with very white eyes peered curiously back at him.

"I don't like the looks of it," Uncle Ray said.

"It looks like they'd rather slit your throat than take you fishing," Tom said.

I had to agree. I'd never, until then, been scared by Mexico, and all of a sudden there I was with stomach flutters.

"Why don't we go ask Señor Alonzo's advice?" I suggested.

There was a spooky silence, like I'd opened the door to a dark, empty room and found Uncle Ray glaring at me from inside. I don't know what Uncle Ray, at that point anyway, could have had against Señor Alonzo. Maybe it was just Mexicans in general that he didn't approve of. But then Ray never acted prejudiced with Mexican-Americans at home. I think it had something to do with the fact that Señor Alonzo was both Mexican and rich.

Finally, though, he just sighed. "Well," he said, "I guess it can't hurt any. He might even know where we can find a good American captain."

Back at the supermarket we found Señor Alonzo taking inventory on some canned goods. He dropped everything when he saw us. "Welcome, my friends!" he said. "I knew I would see you again." Then, turning to me and extending his hand, which I grabbed probably a little faster than decorum called for, he said pleasantly, "Hello, little *muchacho flaco*." I learned later that flaco means skinny, but Señor Alonzo was not trying to make fun of me when he said it, I'm sure.

The way Uncle Ray went on to explain our situation, you would have thought he'd been the one whose idea it was to come to the Señor for advice. I guess that's the way he had to do it because he was a proud man and he liked to appear as if he were on top of every situation, but still it bothered me. Ray once told me, much later, that the important thing in life was to not let yourself be pushed. Maybe that's what it was. Maybe he felt he was being pushed into something and had to push back a little.

I had the distinct impression that he was pushing against me.

Señor Alonzo, however, was very understanding and said that he knew exactly what Uncle Ray meant. He said that he was glad we'd come to him for advice.

"Look," he said, "I know a captain, a personal friend of mine, and he's absolutely dependable. I'll tell you what. I'll take tomorrow morning off and go out with you myself to see that you get some good fishing."

I thought this a fine idea and glanced eagerly at Uncle Ray. I don't believe Uncle Ray thought it so fine, but with Señor Alonzo standing there beaming munificently at us, he could do little besides smile weakly and say that it would certainly be very nice. On the way back to Cabrillo he didn't say much to me.

If it hadn't been for Tom, who loved to play pool, we might have been able to skip the rec hall that night. He wanted badly to go, but not alone. So we all went. It's strange, but that night I got the feeling that we were on separate vacations, Tom and Ray and myself. I had gone to Mexico, but Uncle Ray and Tom had gone someplace else, like to Johnson's Pool Hall on Fourteenth Street back in Compton. They played serious, meaningful pool, just the two of them. I naturally felt left out, which I believe was the idea. Uncle Ray was sore because I'd got him mixed up with Señor Alonzo.

In the morning the Señor was waiting for us down on the docks with about three fishing poles, all different sizes, a folding captain's chair, and a big ice chest. He had a little dirty Mexican boy with him that I knew couldn't be his son because he was so ragged. Señor Alonzo greeted us again in his big, generous way and then he introduced me to Ernie. He said that Ernie was his boy but I think he just meant that he was helping carry all his stuff. Señor Alonzo had never mentioned anything about family. I thought Ernie was okay, but he couldn't speak any English and so we didn't really have much to say to each other. He watched me a lot, but when I looked at him he turned his head away real quick, like he hadn't really been watching at all.

I still had the feeling, a feeling, that would stick with me for the rest of the day, that Uncle Ray was purposely ignoring me.

When we piled into the boat, along with about fifty other Americans, Tom and Uncle Ray, pampering one of Ray's favorite sport-fishing superstitions, grabbed two spaces right at the stern. The name of the boat was *El Bonito*, which Uncle Ray had told me was a kind of a fish, and Señor Alonzo introduced us not only to his captain friend, but to the entire crew of mechanics and deck hands. We were celebrities, more or less. The captain's name, the only one I can remember, was Chet Ramirez. He looked like a good-natured pirate.

"Sorry, Jim," Uncle Ray said to me, "but I guess you'll have to scout a place for yourself. There just isn't any more room back here."

I looked around. There didn't seem to be any spaces left anywhere and I was ready to sit down and forget about fishing when I heard the Señor's voice.

"Hey, *muchacho*," he called. "Come sit here. You and Ernie sit next to me."

The Señor was already settled into his captain's chair. Ernie sat on one side of him and Señor Alonzo patted his hand on a second wooden stool to his other side. *"Aquí.* You sit here."

The sea, I remember, had large rolling swells in it that day, but there was no wind when we started out, so the rolling was soft and smooth. The hills that rose up on shore were brown and dead except for the pale green cactus. I wondered what it would be like if something happened to the boat and we washed up on that dead, barren shore with no food or water. As long as Ensenada was in sight I couldn't make myself get too worried. We would just hike back along the beach to town. Soon, though, we went around a rocky point and Ensenada was no longer in sight. Everyone on the boat became quiet and watched the brown hills move by above the deep green sea. I wondered if they were thinking about what would happen if something went wrong with the boat. Señor Alonzo put his hand reassuringly on my shoulder. It was like he'd been reading my thoughts.

"What do you think of this place, *muchacho*? Beautiful, no?"

"It looks pretty dead," I answered and right away felt stupid. I guess it was sort of beautiful, except that the hills were so brown and lifeless. Señor Alonzo just laughed and I glanced out of the corner of my eyes to see if his belly was laughing too, but I couldn't tell from the side.

Then suddenly the motors stopped. For a moment as we coasted through the swells, there was no sound except for the far-off crashing of breakers and the screeching of the seagulls.

"This is it!" Captain Ramirez yelled.

I glanced up at the cockpit, up above the main cabin, and saw the captain waving his hand across the blue sky.

"Okay to fish!" he called out.

You might have thought there was a fire. The fishermen scurried about waving bare, shimmering fish hooks and crowding in close around the live-bait tank. Fifty minnows soon slapped the water in quick succession, and fifty slightly whiskered faces turned stony with expectation, waiting for the first big strike.

Señor Alonzo, though, just kept gazing at the hills and the blue sky with this faraway look in his eyes.

"Are we going to fish, Señor Alonzo?" I asked politely. I hated to bother him, but people were starting to catch fish already. He blinked his eyes back into focus.

"Oh sure, sure, we'll fish," he said. "In a minute." He pulled the ice chest from under his captain's chair and took a couple of beers out of it. He asked me if I wanted one, but if Uncle Ray saw me drinking a beer he'd skin me, so I said no thanks. He gave one to Ernie and Ernie drank it down just like it was soda pop. I was under the bright morning sun, and not too interested in catching fish, so my mind drifted with the sway of the boat.

It was sort of a swell feeling to be sitting there on that stool next to Señor Alonzo, having him talk to us occasionally and tell us stories about the ocean and the Mexican fishermen. He sure knew a lot more about fishing than I ever would have expected a guy who ran a supermarket to know. He told me about some men farther south along the coast who had completely given up living with other men and made their lives sailing the coastal waters alone in tiny, homemade sailboats. They were completely cut off from civilization and didn't even communicate with each other. I thought that was great and it made me think about my plan to come back down to Mexico by myself some day and live. That'd really be the life, I thought.

Everyone on the boat meanwhile was catching plenty of good big fish. We three, Ernie, me, and Señor Alonzo, caught a few but we spent most of the time talking, especially the Señor. After he had quite a few beers, he started talking louder and louder and laughing more frequently. Ernie was drinking them too, just like Coca-Cola, only the more he drank the quieter he became. Finally I worked up the courage to ask the Señor if Ernie was his son.

"Ernie?" Señor Alonzo said. "No, he's not my son. He's just my boy. He's my good boy." He asked me if I could understand that. I said no I couldn't. I asked him what he meant by "his boy."

"Well, just like you're my boy, too," he said. "My little *muchacho*." He asked me if I could understand that, but again I had to tell him no.

Well, instead of trying to explain any further, the Señor just made a backhand swipe, like brushing bugs away, but actually what he was brushing away were words, and he put his big arms around me and Ernie and hugged us both close to him. I could feel his strength. I twisted my head to see if Uncle Ray and Tom were watching but they were somewhere up in the front of the boat. Poor Ernie looked miserable, like he was getting sick.

"You're such damn good boys," the Señor was saying. "That's all I'm telling you.

"Sure you are. All I've ever asked of God, just two good little *muchachos* to take fishing and tell stories, how simple, no? What then do I have? I have little girls, two of them." Señor Alonzo seemed suddenly unhappy.

"Where are they?" I asked. "Why didn't they come with you?"

"They are at home," the Señor said. "They are frightened of the sea."

Señor Alonzo fairly spat the last words from his mouth, as if their taste were unpleasant.

"Two good boys like you: healthy, strong boys, that's what I should have. But no, no, nothing is simple...."

His voice trailed off and when I looked up at his face to see where it had gone I found instead real tears in his eyes. Without warning, a hot rush of something that resembled anger welled inside me as I began to realize Señor Alonzo was pressing me into a relationship I wasn't sure I wanted to be part of. It was like a jolt. The hot feeling came and passed, and without knowing exactly why I felt sort of empty. Ernie was making funny sounds like he was crying and he whined something in Spanish. The Señor let him go and Ernie leaned over the side of the boat and started to throw up. He must have been really sick because he kept throwing up for about twenty minutes.

After that Señor Alonzo didn't tell us any more stories or even talk to us very much.

He became sullen and he drank a lot more beer, until it was all gone. He must have had about fifteen bottles of it. Ernie just sat on his stool and looked miserable and the Señor slouched in his captain's chair and became more drunk. I hated to see him like that, all crumpled and morose. He sat there without moving for a long time and finally, just as the sun was becoming unbearably hot, Captain Ramirez told everyone to get their lines in because we were heading back.

I was glad. I wanted to get off the boat.

A school of dolphin escorted us part of the way back to Ensenada. When you looked over the side of the boat down into the water you could see their black forms moving along like shadows. They were so graceful, it looked like they weren't even using any effort to swim. I watched them for a long time and tried to get Señor Alonzo interested but he just sat in his chair. When we docked, Captain Ramirez and some of the Mexican deck hands had to help him off the boat. He was awfully drunk, and I guess they didn't want him falling into the harbor. We were the last ones to get off, along with Tom and Uncle Ray, whom I'd hardly seen all morning. Just long enough to notice that they had more fish than we could eat in two months.

"What's wrong with him?" Uncle Ray asked me. I knew that if I told him the Señor was drunk, Ray would say he'd been right all along about Mexicans, especially rich ones.

"I guess he's seasick," I said. I felt lousy because I had to lie.

Señor Alonzo had waved the deck hands away from him and was standing above us on the dock, his arms outstretched and his palms upturned, as if to receive rays from the sun. Everyone left in the boat, which included me and Ernie, Tom and Uncle Ray, Captain Ramirez and some of the crew, all looked up at him and waited.

"My friends," he began. His voice sounded deep and vibrant but far away, like a thunderstorm that's passed. "My friends, I wish to thank you all for this very beautiful day we have spent together with our Mother the sea. We have been within her fertile womb and we have reaped the harvest of her abundant garden and it is important that we have done this together, my friends. We have gorged on her generous offerings and as we leave with our harvest to return to her Brother the earth we must remember that it is in the sea that life has its roots. Thank you for this day and go with God, my friends."

The crew stood silently with heads bowed until the Señor was done, then they hopped up on the deck and trooped by him solemnly in a line, and each man shook hands warmly with him. Ernie and I shook his hand too, and as we went by he looked at us and bit his upper lip. He held both of our hands in his for a long time and I thought he was going to cry but he didn't.

Standing there, the anger hit me once again, confused, like a momentary flash of heat whose source you can't see. It glowed for a minute and died.

The Señor was still holding our hands when his wife called out to him. She was gliding toward us along the wooden planking that led out from the shore to the fishing boats, the Señor's two daughters flanking her.

"Porfirio!" she called out, waving.

The Señor dropped our hands and turned obediently. His wife quickened her step, and when she arrived I saw that she was an American, rather skinny and plain-faced. She had a kind of eroded elegance, like some aging movie star.

"Porfirio," she said, "we all decided to come down and see you."

"Hullo, Bess," Señor Alonzo said. He smiled, but I could tell that it was a smile of face only because the belly showed no happiness. His little girls were watching me. They were very nicely dressed in pretty skirts and blouses, but their faces were pale and drawn with a kind of homely sadness. I was trying not to stare when all of a sudden Uncle Ray bumped me from behind with the sackful of fish he was dragging and asked if I was ready to go.

" 'Scuse us, ma'am," he said to Mrs. Alonzo when he noticed her. Then he turned around and whispered angrily at me: "Come on, let's get out of here." But the Señor stopped us before we could get away.

Señor Beauregard," he said formally, "I would like to introduce you to my wife and two lovely daughters."

The Señor tried hard to be gallant about the whole thing but his face was strained. I certainly didn't miss the irony in the emphasis he put on "lovely." The spooky part, though, is that I think the Señor himself did. It was like he was trying to convince himself that they really were lovely.

We all shook hands ceremoniously.

"Go with God, my friends," the Señor said to us. He took a girl in each hand and started walking down the wooden planking toward the shore. He walked rigidly like a soldier and with great dignity, but occasionally he leaned a little too far to one side and he had to catch himself from falling.

"Yech!" Tom said when the Señor and his family were well out of hearing. "Were those girls ugly or what."

"Oh, they weren't all *that* bad," Uncle Ray kind of chuckled. "Wasn't his wife a dish?"

Well, that was past the limit; Tom and Uncle Ray just cracked up.

"C'mon," Uncle Ray told me, still erupting with little hiccupped chuckles, "let's get busy cleaning these fish."

It must have been past noon because I was hungry. Maybe that put me on edge.

Anyway, when I told Tom and Uncle Ray about Ernie they said

"Who?" like I was talking Greek. I said skip it. I still don't know where Ernie came from. There were so many dirty little boys in rags who hang around the sport fishing docks in Ensenada hoping for some job and a few pesos, and Ernie might have been one of them. When we walked away from the boat I saw Ernie on his hands and knees with some of the crew, scrubbing down the decks and cleaning her up. Maybe that was his job. I waved, but he merely stared, and I believe that was the first time in my life that the realization of being well-off made me feel bad.

The next day, while Tom and Uncle Ray fished some more on the beach, I rode the breakers and lay in the warm sand dreaming about coming back down to Mexico some day to live. I'd just have a car, or maybe a truck with a camper, and I'd do a lot of traveling around. When we started north the following morning, on our way back to the States, I made mental notes about all the rutted side roads I'd explore and all the little broken-down restaurants where I'd stop and eat hot, spicy food. I hadn't thought of Señor Alonzo for a couple of days, and I never expected to see him again.

By evening we were only halfway to the border from Ensenada because Uncle Ray kept stopping to fish from the rocky points that jutted into the Pacific. When he decided we'd better stop for the night in a hotel, we found one that was called the Rosarito Beach Resort and it was really all right. It had red tile roofing and white adobe walls and shiny brick floors the color of hot coals. We got a nice room and cleaned ourselves up for a real Mexican dinner in the dining room of the resort.

"Do you think the food is safe here?" Tom asked.

"If it wasn't safe in a place like this they'd have a million lawsuits on their hands," Uncle Ray said. This was going to be the first food we'd eaten that we hadn't brought down ourselves, except for some of the fish we'd caught.

Like I said, I never expected to see Señor Alonzo again, but when we were shown to our table who should be sitting next to us but the Señor himself. He smiled a huge and true smile, his belly once again a part of it.

"Welcome, my friends!" he said. When he tried to get up to greet us, he began tottering dangerously and had to sit back down. I knew that he was drunk again. There was a woman with him, a dark Mexican who wore lots of make-up and bright red lipstick and whose dress came down so low in front that when she moved in a certain way her nipples showed.

"May I introduce Señorita Trouvera," the Señor said graciously. It was the first and only time in my entire life that I've ever seen my Uncle Ray shake, actually shake, with the effort to subdue his anger. I thought surely the Señorita would see it, but she just smiled a greeting as if nothing were wrong. I noticed that her teeth looked brown and rotten. She didn't smile with her teeth after that, but only with her lips.

"You will join us for a drink, my friends?" Señor Alonzo offered. "No, thank you," Uncle Ray said coolly, "we're going to eat dinner."

"My friends!" the Señor said indignantly, "one drink will increase your appetite ten times over. We will have a drink together."

He called for the waiter, a little Mexican man with a black waxy mustache and a white jacket that was too big for him.

"Rum and coke for my friend the Señor and coke for the *muchachos*. Two more for the Señorita and I, Julio. You're a good man, Julio."

Julio disappeared and Señor Alonzo returned his attention to us. He scooted his table up next to ours so that I was sitting right next to him. "Hey, we caught fish the other day, didn't we? Didn't we, *muchacho*?" He winked at me and smiled, then put his arm around my shoulder. "Sure we did," the Señor said. "Sure we caught fish. You and me and Ernie. One day, *muchacho*, the Señorita here will be my wife and we'll have so many sons that I'll be able to take different ones fishing every day of the week. We will have big healthy *hijos* who like to fish with their Papa."

I felt it rising again, the small fury I couldn't understand. My eyes were stinging. "Many children yes," the Señorita pronounced slowly and carefully. Uncle Ray seemed to have passed into a kind of paralysis.

"Well, and how is Mrs. Alonzo?" I asked. It took me a minute to realize that the voice I heard was my own. It sounded as if it belonged to some boy I'd never met. It was tinged with bitterness. Maybe that's what surprised me.

The Señor stopped smiling immediately. He spread his hands out on the table and stared down at them for a minute, as though counting fingers, then looked up again.

"Mrs. Alonzo? She's fine, of course." His voice sounded brash and unconvincing.

"She's doing very well, really. Did I just say ... I was only pulling your legs of course. You've met my wife; my daughters: they're lovely, no? Of course. Why would I be getting married? It makes no sense. I often tell myself, Porfirio, you make no sense when you are drunk. I become silly. You must excuse, really."

Señorita Trouvera pooched out her lip and frowned at him as the drinks came.

As we sat there drinking the Señor talked and talked, as if he were afraid that once he stopped talking there would be a big silence. He talked, and suddenly about twenty Mexicans with violins came trooping onto the dance floor in front of us. Most of them had little black waxy mustaches like the waiter with the white coat that was too big for him. Señor Alonzo seemed very pleased.

"Chartulio!" he yelled at one of the men with violins. "Chartulio, come over and meet my friends." Chartulio came over. I think he was the leader of the group because he had on a white dinner jacket with a red rose on the lapel and all the other men had on black coats and no roses. He looked a little embarrassed but he was very gracious when the Señor introduced us all. He smelled like butchwax and perfume.

"I did not know that you and the boys were playing here," the Señor said.

"They pay the money and we must play where the money is," said Chartulio, indicating with a sweep of his hand the dining room full of Americans. Then he said: "Of course I am not referring to you, my friends. Porfirio Alonzo's friends are my friends as well."

"Chartulio, I will give you some good advice: play as if there were no Americans in the room. Play as if you were at the club on Lake Chapala. Remember those times, Chartulio? Play your best, and even if no one else will hear it, I will hear it."

"You are right, Porfirio. I told my boys to think of the money. They do not like playing here either, so close to the border." Then to Uncle Ray and Tom and me he said formally: "I hope you will enjoy the music." He gave a neat little bow and rejoined his troupe. I couldn't help but like him.

"Americans usually don't like the music Chartulio plays," the Señor explained. "And he's getting old and set in his ways. He will not change his music but always plays the old songs."

A small Mexican with a high, excited voice introduced the group as the Violins de Mexico. People looked up and clapped politely, then returned to their dinners and conversations. The Violins de Mexico began playing and it sounded like some of the music I'd been hearing on the radio the past couple of days. Sometimes it was sort of happy and lilting, then it would become sad. I thought it was very pretty music and I felt good about enjoying it because I knew that Chartulio would be pleased that an American liked his music. I turned and was going to tell Señor Alonzo how much I liked it but I stopped when I saw the look on his face: there was sorrow in his eyes, and large tears were making shiny tracks down his cheeks. At one place, right at the height of a crescendo, the violins hit this sort of melancholy minor key and Señor Alonzo closed his eyes and bit his lip. He shook his head slowly back and forth.

"Beautiful, Chartulio," he whispered. "Chapala, Chartulio, remember Chapala." Those twenty men stood in the middle of the dance floor and played their hearts out while people at the tables talked and laughed among themselves and ate their dinners. They played for a long time and not once during that time did a single muscle in Uncle Ray's face so much as twitch. When the music finally stopped there was a terrible silence for a moment until the people realized that the musicians weren't playing any longer. Then there was a scattering of applause and the violinists stood with great dignity in the center of the dance floor and made big sweeping bows. It was awful. They deserved better than they were getting.

I was clapping a little louder than most of the people, but Señor Alonzo, sitting beside me, was creating a regular thunder with those huge hands of his. His lips were drawn into a tight line across his face. People were beginning to stare at him when all at once he stood up very straight and tall, but none too steadily, and clapped even louder. His face was gravely sober when he nudged me with his leg and made a jerk of his head to indicate that I was to stand up with him. I glanced at Uncle Ray and it wasn't too pleasant to see the look he had for me. Then I looked back out at those violinists standing there proudly as what little applause there was died away. I made my decision. I stood up with Señor Alonzo and kept on clapping.

The Señor glanced down at me. He was smiling now but there were tears in his eyes.

"The music was beautiful, was it not, my son?"

I nodded my head and watched the violinists file quickly out of the room in the same direction from which they had come.

In a minute Chartulio came back over to our table with a large drink in his hand. He sat down and took a large swig of it, then wiped his forehead with a handkerchief.

"Ah, Porfirio, they do not like the old songs," he said hopelessly.

"Who cares about them," said the Señor. "I will listen to your music always."

"Sure, Porfirio, but they pay the money and we must play for those who pay the money."

"I have the money also," Señor Alonzo said indignantly. "I will pay the money to hear your songs, the old songs."

"But you are only one, Porfirio, you are only one and they are many. There must be many to pay the money." Chartulio took another long drink.

"I like your music, Chartulio," I said. "I thought it was pretty." Chartulio glanced at me, a little surprised.

"I am glad," he said kindly. "Now there are two. But, you see, there must be many, and even thrice two would not be enough. But I am glad you liked the music. Who is this *muchacho*, Porfirio?"

"He's one of my boys," the Señor said.

"He's a good boy to like such music."

"Yes, he's a good boy."

Uncle Ray got up quickly and excused us and said that we had to be going.

The Bright World of Dandelion Court

1.

This story may have begun before Old Major Tom Keenan was even on the planet, when the Dandelion neighborhood was still meadows and forests at the northern end of the state, at the eastern edge of the now-sprawling city, just past the beltway that encircled roughly two million people. Before the tree-crunchers and the earth scrapers began making streams as straight as a road across the plains, and before the civil engineers came and the surveyors' stakes and yellow ribbons flapped in the summer breeze, marking off one piece of the world from its neighbor, the likes of Tom Keenan had not been seen, nor did he yet exist.

Dandelion Court, which joined Dandelion Lane, which in turn flowed into Dandelion Street, like Chinese nesting eggs, all the same but of different sizes, in fact had been what today's environmentalists refer to as wetlands but which were then simply called swamps. Through this swamp ran a lumber-mill railroad track that crossed a trestle high above the once pristine creek. The crunchers and scrapers destroyed what was there and then in-filled the land with untold tons of rocks, gravel, and muddy earth.

From out of this primordial swamp, eventually, came the neighborly cul-de-sac known as Dandelion Court, throughout which nary a dandelion was ever seen. And eventually, along came Old Major Tom Keenan, who was neither old nor a major.

2.

One time, just the other day, in fact, Old Major Tom Keenan sat on the backyard deck watching as the shadows grew eastward and the afternoon turned to evening. He remembered that it was the Fourth of July seven years ago to the day when he and his ex-wife Diana sat in just the same place, trying to get comfortable in their old directors' chairs, while they watched the glow and fire to the south, over the city that they had just left in order to inhabit the single-level and unremarkable house at 2214 Dandelion Court. The distant fiery haloes and sparkling shards of fire followed by mushrooming clouds of smoke seemed to Tom to resemble a nuclear attack, but somewhere far away, such as eastern China or some city in Florida.

Sometime in between their first summer as residents of Dandelion Court seven years ago and just-the-other-day, the Keenans sat outside, as usual, on the Day of Independence. It just happened to be one of the coldest Fourths of July on record, 59 degrees Fahrenheit with a light drizzle.

Diana, chilled, went back into the comfortable living room, and Tom followed shortly. Inside the house with matching sofa covers and wallpaper, Tom's hopes for the future, but not his love for Diana, died right there on the recently vacuumed tight-weave beige carpet when Diana said she would like to leave the marriage. That the day happened to be Independence Day Tom did not consider until the first anniversary of their divorce.

3.

"It's always too late to start over," said Major Tom Keenan one sunny afternoon when he sat outside on his deck talking to Neighbor Jack, who had just bought a new Pomeranian puppy for himself and Glynda. Deer commonly traversed the neighborhood when they emerged from the forested park just beyond the development's boundaries. Jack and Glynda's departed little Misty had been trampled and cut to shreds by the cloven hooves of a protective black-tailed doe that Misty barked at the way she barked at anything that moved. Jack held the new dog, Shelley, gently, protectively, in his right arm as he set his beer can down on the coaster.

"Do you mean, it's never too late to start over?" Jack asked. Major Tom was in one of his moods.

"No, I meant that it's always too late to start over," Tom insisted. "Even when you're young. Once, before Diana divorced me, I thought I was still young enough to enjoy being old. But now I'm too old to enjoy anything."

Jack responded carefully, keeping in mind that Old Tom was only 58. "Maybe you'd like to have a dog," Jack suggested. "A companion—some company, a loyal friend."

Major Tom responded thoughtfully, to Neighbor Jack's surprise, with, "What kind of dog?"

"What kind do you want? There are all kinds at the Humane Society shelter."

Major Tom then thought about what would happen to the dog if he, Major Tom Keenan, died before the dog died. He couldn't stand the thought of abandoning an animal like that. When he explained his concern to Neighbor Jack, Jack suggested, "Well, why don't you get an old dog. Maybe he'll die about the same time you do."

Jack was a good neighbor.

"That's a good idea," said Major Tom. And that's how Neighbor Jack agreed to help his friend find just the right dog.

4.

Old Major Tom was turning 58 on Tuesday. Time was not only passing more quickly, Tom mused, but the rate of time's acceleration seemed to have increased as well.

Jack and Glynda invited Major Tom over that Tuesday for a special birthday dinner and managed to surprise him with a red, white, and blue cake, an amateurishly done emblem of some kind of medal honoring Old Tom positioned roughly in the center of the frosted top layer.

Also surprising was that Old Tom's ex-wife Diana and her current husband Tim were in attendance. When Old Tom caught Jack's eye, it simply rolled in a "you don't want to know" way. It was agreed between Old Tom and Neighbor Jack that Diana had not chosen her second husband well.

It was a sunny, crisp day in the autumn before the summer of Old Tom's misfortune, and after a little awkwardness among spouses and ex- or currently in-favor spouses, the five of them walked down to the clean suburban cemetery to admire the autumn leaves on the maturing yet not fully developed oaks, maples, and other hardwood species that had so far been spared the impact of deadly plagues destroying entire forests around the country. For more than an hour they read inscriptions, most of them relatively recent, because this place was still too new for most of its inhabitants to have been buried in these graves. They were still alive in the Dandelion neighborhood.

5.

Winter and Spring passed through the Dandelion suburb almost like afterthoughts. On a Sunday in what was suddenly July, during the summer of Tom's life that we are considering, the shadows from the sun setting behind the green trees that surrounded Dandelion Court almost took everything with them. Tom felt the sensation of free-fall into the void. Both the sun and Tom Keenan's mood were in steep decline. It may be that the dog lying beside Tom's chair felt Old Tom's malaise.

The dog and Major Tom had met on this very day, a cloudless smog-free beauty with a light breeze whispering from the north. Neighbor Jack had left precious Shelley at home with Glynda and taken Tom to a Humane Society shelter a ways out past the Dandelion neighborhood. Jack had bought a brand-new Japanese hybrid car, one of the first to hit the American market, and he wanted Tom to ride in it.

So it was that Neighbor Jack and Old Major Tom Keenan pulled silently out of Dandelion Court in Jack's hybrid, turned down Dandelion Lane to Dandelion Street, and finally onto Division Avenue, all the way to the dam, which was the reason that the Dandelion and other downstream flood-plain communities could enjoy not being flooded every three or four years. It was a modestly proportioned dam, retaining a long recreational reservoir, from which issued what became a shallow river in the late summer and autumn, perfect for inner-tubing.

Tom had not been thinking of the dog. He was brooding over his sense that he wasn't as important to other people—notably, Diana—as he'd once believed. This was not a depressing thought, but a clarifying distinction between the real world and the world he perceived to be real. With a few exceptions, people in general didn't give a damn about Old Major Tom Keenan. But neither did they wish him ill.

Neighbor Jack's new hybrid car was as road-noisy as Tom's new Ford Fiesta, but Tom kept that observation to himself.

"Rides pretty clean," Major Tom said, not knowing what to say that didn't express an opinion on the quality of the ride. He was happy that Neighbor Jack felt good and expansive about driving a car that he believed was both peppy and good on fuel efficiency.

As these things go, Major Tom recalled riding in the back seat of his parents' car when he was nine or ten, traveling through western American states, in the mountains and alongside heartbreakingly clear rivers. They drove the old two-lane highways where you could just pull over to the side of the road, get out of the car, and stand in the river until your feet were frozen, then pull out a basket of sandwiches and eat them right there without a single car going by.

Jack pulled in and parked at the Humane Society shelter, and they entered a dim place filled with echoing, deafening noise that had the exact opposite effect the yowling dogs really wanted to demonstrate—that they were lovable and available.

Hudson was in the last kennel on the right, curled down in a far corner on the cement floor. He was the only non-barking dog in the room. When he looked up at Tom by raising his eyes without lifting his head, Old Major Tom was struck dumb with love.

Hudson had been waiting all his life, or so it seemed, for Tom Keenan to come along.

One could pretty accurately describe Hudson as a handsome, arthritic, slightly shy dog who never barked. Of medium size, weighing 35 pounds, fur sand-colored and smooth, Hudson moved his body like a tank. The musculature around his forehead, eyes, and skull had atrophied somewhat, giving him a haunted look. The staff told Tom that Hudson was nine or ten, and healthy.

Tom adopted him on the spot, and the three of them returned to Dandelion Court, Hudson riding in the front passenger seat of Neighbor Jack's car, and Tom in the back, where there was a surprisingly generous amount of leg room for a hybrid compact.

When Tom brought Hudson into his local veterinarian for a look-over, Doc Hotch guessed his age more like fourteen or fifteen. Tom Keenan didn't care. He had found what he didn't even know he was looking for: a quiet old dog with nothing better to do than grow on Tom's heart.

Tom's psychiatrist told Tom how pleased she was. "That's a very positive step," she said.

And that is how Tom checked his descent into the void on that beautiful summer evening as he sat watching the shadows sweep everything, except himself, and his dog Hudson, into darkness. To all who knew Old Major Tom Keenan, it was clear as gin that Tom's new old dog, the shepherd mutt with soulful eyes who flinched whenever Tom or anyone reached out to pet him, was the best thing that could have happened to their good neighbor.

6.

Old Major Tom Keenan took his early morning walk with Hudson through the woodland that still extended beyond his home to the west. This was also the unofficial path to the cemetery, used regularly by joggers, dog walkers, and cyclists.

A few hardy runners passed him in the early morning gloom, and in between such encounters what was later identified as a Barred Owl swooped twice, barely missing Tom's head. Tom didn't hear anything the first time, just felt a hair-raising breeze pass quickly over his head. Hudson either didn't notice or didn't care. Then the sound came: *flu-up, flu-up, flu-up,* and the enormous motion of extended wings took the owl back into the trees.

Tom later described the owl as nearsighted, because, as he told the story to Neighbor Jack over an uncharacteristic serving of distilled spirits around nine in the morning, "It took the damned thing two passes to figure out I wasn't on the menu."

Tom regretted his thoughts—thankfully left unspoken—when Neighbor Jack's dog Misty was mauled: "That's just how Nature works, pal; survival of the fittest," Tom had thought. But somewhere in this under-story of Nature there yet lurked surprises, often dark and bloody, that Tom sensed even this morning.

Jack had said to Tom after Misty's misfortune that he had no idea that deer could kill a dog, even a small one like Misty.

"It's not the size," Major Tom said.

Neighbors Bud and Bea Friday, for example, owned, and fed, a pair of sweet-natured Rottweilers, Gus and Rose, brother and sister. Tom reminded Neighbor Jack that the Rotties were large but apparently tolerant of just about any creature, with little of what the dog people call prey-drive. The big dogs were so friendly and easy-going that everyone living in Dandelion Court loved them. The Fridays took Gus and Rose everywhere with them, nearly 400 pounds of dog sitting in the bed of a black crew-cab Toyota Tundra.

The day of the swooping incident, Major Tom called the parks department and reported the incident to a county functionary who seemed barely awake. He thanked Tom for the report, and said if he heard anything else of a similar nature occurring, the County would investigate.

"I think you ought to shoot those owls," said Tom before hanging up.

Turning to Neighbor Jack, he said, "It's like Nature was turning against us."

"Yes," he repeated after a thoughtful pause, "Just like Nature was turning against us."

7.

"If I was happy, and thought and felt only the pleasurable parts of life," thought Major Tom one day, "if I was, say, normal, if that's what people normally feel, life wouldn't seem so interesting and heartbreaking as it actually is."

At around seven o'clock on a late-July evening, Major Tom was jolted from his thoughts by a call from Laurie Shortt, whose house was next to Bud and Bea Friday's on Dandelion Court. Tom had been barely paying attention to a crime scene investigation show on his television but realized the sound he heard was not the TV, but the Doppler-effect approach of an emergency aid car siren.

As the story was told later, Bud Friday was at home watching baseball in his sports chair when he felt his chest constrict with agonizing force. He managed to dial 9-1-1 on the phone next to him before falling unconscious, while his wife Bea wandered from room to room, frightened and not sure where she'd left her knitting. Bud's agonized moan as he fell was heard by Laurie, who rushed over to help.

Tom came out to see the EMTs rushing into the house, the lights of their trucks casting a blinding hypnotic glare around this epicenter of commotion. After only a few minutes, the techs carried Bud Friday out of the barn-red one-story rambler on a foldable transom that wheeled into the back of the aid car like a well-made drawer sliding quietly into the cabinet. Bea was helped into the aid car front seat.

And then the Fridays, Bud and Bea, two fine neighbors and longtime homeowners who lived good years in Dandelion Court, were gone.

Tom Keenan didn't hear much about them after that. Bud and Bea's son was seen occasionally at the house, evidently having been put in charge of the estate, and Tom had a feeling that he would never see Bud or Bea again, that even if Bud survived they would be in a nursing home and they would never get out alive.

Laurie had stayed in the Friday house with Gus and Rose that night. Major Tom tried to sleep, but heard the muffled whimpering of Gus and Rose from across the street far into the early morning.

At 3:30 a.m., feeling suddenly and completely alone, Major Tom called Diana, but got her voicemail after only one ring and realized that she had turned her phone off for the night. Tom fell asleep with the phone sitting on his chest. Now and then, had anyone been listening, they would have heard Old Major Tom Keenan mumble once or twice in his sleep:

"Gone, just like that."

8.

The Dandelion Court citizens found some levity in the wake of Bud's cardiac "event" when they heard about Tom's new girlfriend, who happened to be a 19-year-old sorrel mare, about thirteen and a half hands tall. Her name was Lady Jane, and Tom, during his first lesson at the Sweetwater Stables just a few miles farther out from the beltway, took to calling her just Lady.

"When are you going to bring that girl home so she can meet your neighbors?" Neighbor Jack teased Major Tom, who was sorry he'd ever told the story of his horse riding lessons. "Hudson must be jealous," Jack said, wagging a finger.

At an ethnic-food potluck dinner party hosted by Phoebe and Glenn Stowe, Tom responded to the teasing by saying how Lady Jane was much smarter than he was. "I learn something new every week, and I feel so connected!" Tom immediately wished he hadn't used that word. *Connected* described a terrible state of isolation created by digital telecommunications companies trying to connect you to everything, all the time. A better word than *connected*, he thought, might have been *happy*.

"This horse whispering stuff, I don't know," said Tom to Glen and Phoebe. "A horse is a complicated animal. But I talk to her and ride as well as I can, and she makes me feel, well, like I've got a friend."

The Stowes just didn't get it, Tom realized, so he stopped talking. The conversations around them became silent, as though everyone had been talking together in groups but were actually listening to Tom Keenan. After an awkward pause, Laurie's daughter, who Laurie had on weekends and who was helping out in the kitchen, somehow got a piece of silverware stuck in the garbage disposal, sending up a painfully grating racket. Phoebe Stowe screamed about her grandmother's silverware being ruined and ran to the kitchen. That offered Tom a chance to move to the front door, and out.

Major Tom never talked about horses again, except for once, when he told Diana on the phone about his riding and Lady Jane and how it made him feel so good. As at the party, he felt a bit foolish, but also heard his ex-wife crying softly at the other end of the line. "What's wrong?" Tom asked.

"Nothing is wrong," she said. "I think it's beautiful."

Diana was genuinely happy that her ex-husband, the Horse Whisperer, had enjoyed a brush with happiness.

9.

As time passed that pleasant, promising summer, Old Major Tom and his dog Hudson settled into a nice daily routine that is, to some, the best part of living with a dog. Tom was up at six a.m., out the door at 6:15 and around the Dandelion neighborhood by himself, then back by 6:45 to roust Hudson, feed man and dog and, at seven, walk with Hudson down the cemetery path, then back home where Tom made himself a second cup of coffee. And so on throughout the day, with lots of improvisation after these essential beginnings.

On his walks, Tom liked to say "Hello" or "Good morning" to any neighbor who was up and outside at this hour. Few in this community of the retired, disabled, or those who simply liked the feel of the place and had found a home at a good price, were to be seen before seven.

Old Tom very badly missed Diana, who as their time together through the years passed uneventfully and childlessly, realized that she could not provide Tom with what he needed. That was much more than she could give anyone. Whenever, as a moody divorced man, Tom felt himself sinking toward the bottom of the lake, his first impulse was to call Diana, but not wanting to pester her, he usually ended up calling Neighbor Jack so that Jack could tell him reasonable things.

On one such day, however, Old Tom connected only to Jack's voicemail. Deciding not to leave a message, he instead dialed Diana's number.

Her new husband Tim (Old Tom thought of him as "new" even though they had been married for three years now) answered the phone. Tom was unable to speak at first. It wasn't that Tim made him feel uneasy or feel anything at all. It was just that he had expected to hear Diana's voice. After a pause, Tom Keenan said, "Hi Tim. Tom Keenan here."

"Major Tom!" Tim responded brightly. "Good to hear from you!"

Tom disliked it when Tim, or anyone outside the circle of Dandelion Court, used his honorific title. The way Tim said the words made Tom think of chutney. Major Tom's Chutney.

Tim Japer then told Tom the most amazing story.

It seems, began Tim, that Diana had a sister living in Mexico who Tom had never known existed. Anyway, this was according to Tim. Because her sister had, apparently inadvertently, been responsible for the death of her ten-month-old son Carlos, the child's father—Diana's sister's boyfriend, a Mexican bus tour guide—had endeavored, unsuccessfully, said Tim with something that sounded only vaguely like relief, to have Diana's sister convicted of murder.

A million questions banged together in Tom's mind. Primarily, he wanted to know why Diana had never told him of this sister, and if she had, why he had not remembered it.

"And this in a Catholic country," Tim said, without explaining what that meant.

Old Major Tom Keenan took a deep breath. He no longer felt the heavy gloom of a midnight soul. But he felt the wing-flutter of astonishment at this remarkable piece of information. Simply hanging the phone up took effort because Tom needed to know more, but he didn't want it from Tim Japer. Diana had a sister who was a child murderer, inadvertently?

Life, Major Tom thought, as he often did, can be a curious endeavor.

10.

But it wasn't true. Diana and Major Tom were walking down the tree-shaded street near a suburban-mall Starbuck's close to where Diana worked for an outdoor equipment manufacturer in the marketing department.

When asked about Tim's story, Diana told Major Tom that the

only reason she had come to Neighbor Jack and Glynda's house earlier that summer for his birthday was that she wanted to see Tom, not knowing how to avoid bringing Tim, whose current psychosis involved making up stories about imaginary family members.

This made Old Tom feel great relief. He was glad that the story wasn't true, at least. But he wondered about Tim.

"So," Tom tried to summarize, "you do not have a secret murderer-sister."

"No," Diana told him, "only a sociopath husband." Then she cried a little, and then they kissed, but not for very long. Diana was waiting for a call from corporate and had to get back to work.

11.

Like God, Major Tom found that within a few days of creating something—God the Universe, Tom his renewable sense of self—he became bored and lonely, rubbing up against his real or perceived failures like a purring cat. In Major Tom's world, there were no major players, no go-to guy, no leading men, only a collection of bit parts and cameos. Tom had always been satisfied playing the small supporting roles. Even with Hudson and, once weekly, Lady Jane to soothe the wounded parts of him, Tom suffered.

And so it was that Tom was wakened one morning, a morning that would become a pleasant July day, by a dream he had. Hudson was still curled up in his cloth and lambskin bed, and did not usually awaken before his seven o'clock foray.

Tom was able to close his eyes and build a clear memory of the dream, in which he tried to explain to Diana the difference between the Tao Te Ching and an 82-year-old Douglas fir tree in his back yard. Diana didn't get it. Tom's longing for his ex-wife alternated with the urge to strangle her in pure frustration. Easing back into the dream, sensing the warm glow of near-enlightenment, Major Tom suddenly knew exactly the difference between the Tao Te Ching and the Douglas fir tree in his back yard. Hah! No difference! Big Zen joke!

In his dream, Tom looked out the back window at the fir tree, which suddenly fell or rather disintegrated, spewing beetles into the air, some pelting against the window.

It had seemed so real.

Later that morning, Major Tom received a call from Laurie

Shortt, who reported that Bud Friday had passed sometime before dawn after lying in a coma for the better part of two weeks. Services were being planned. Bea's future was pending; she was living temporarily at her son-in-law's house somewhere nearby.

Major Tom considered what Bud Friday had said recently about making a run for a seat on the city council, since nobody else seemed able to do the job right.

"Sometimes," said Bud, "you've just got to set fire to your boat and push it out to sea."

Bud would have made a damn fine city councilman, thought Old Major Tom Keenan.

What Tom Keenan wasn't thinking about, however, because he didn't know, was that Gus and Rose, the Rottweilers, had gone missing.

12.

On a Sunday morning in mid-August, here is how Major Tom Keenan ended up not going to church.

A few hours earlier he had been on the phone with his brother Mike, who was trying to talk Old Tom out of pulling the trigger, downing the pills, or doing whatever it was this time. Mike always encouraged his brother to seek help, and Tom did go so far as to meet with a psychiatrist a few times. However, the appropriate antidepressant medication continued to elude him, and he had tried many.

Tom very much disliked the crisis lines: strangers trying to help were to be avoided like a hornet's nest. Mike Keenan did what he could manage from a distance, but rarely visited because his two boys and his wife were uneasy around Old Tom.

"I really know what the bottom feels like," Tom told his brother in a doleful voice. "I can see where a person wants to stop living."

Mike had never been depressed a day in his life, Old Major Tom sulked to himself.

Out of patience, Mike suggested that his brother call his psychiatrist, Dr. White, if he felt this was a crisis. But Tom didn't like to bother doctors or other important people on weekends. He felt that his problems could wait until Monday, and of course when Monday came, what had been a crisis the day before couldn't even be brought to mind by Major Tom.

"Or go find a church. It's Sunday after all. That's what people do."

Tom had never found a church to suit him, so he stayed home for the day, fixing what he could fix, watching bits and pieces of a pointless midseason baseball game, and walking Hudson through the park.

13.

Comedy is the intersection of ambition and stupidity, decided Major Tom Keenan one day, after listening to the preposterously self-serving radio news and gossip program "Sunz and Baker" on PeoplePlus Radio, AM 740, then reviving some of his own most rueful or embarrassing acts or words. He switched the dial to another station.

Neighbor Jack came over a little later and they sat in Tom Keenan's living room where they drank coffee and listened to Rush Limbaugh on the radio tell his audience that Michael J. Fox was faking his Parkinson's disease whenever he went on television.

"I don't think he's faking it," averred Neighbor Jack. "My cousin has Parkinson's disease and she says that wild movement he does is actually a side effect of the medicine."

But Tom's mind was elsewhere.

The closer you were to death—your own or someone else's, Tom was thinking—the more you began to notice an eerie synchronicity in the manner and order in which things occurred.

Tom said to Jack, "I had this cat once. Actually, it was Diana's cat, but he lived with me when she left. He got into some antifreeze or something and died within a few days—horrible death. But I remember the first few nights after he died, I saw his form move across the dark bedroom after I turned the lights out. And I could actually feel his weight settle into the bed in his familiar spot next to my feet."

Neighbor Jack, after nodding at Tom's story, said they should go practice their tee shots at the driving range. Neither of them golfed much, but they enjoyed hitting the balls and seeing who could drive the farthest.

"I think," Old Major Tom continued, disregarding Jack's suggestion, "that the sorts of thing we see as the exceptions, the miracles, are not coincidental but happen all the time. We're just not tuned into that frequency most of the time, so we don't notice."

"For Bud," Jack said. "Bud would have wanted us to go outside and hit some balls.

"Okay," said Tom, getting up to go dig out his clubs. As Tom often concluded his conversations with Jack, he added, "Life is certainly strange."

14.

The day of the accident began with the usual routine. It was Tom's riding day, but Lady Jane has sustained a minor hoof injury, so Tom had to improvise and decided to walk the park trail, which followed the course of the once-defiled creek, sticking to the border of the cemetery, eventually reaching a commercial and retail part of town; this was Tom's destination. It was Monday midday, and Hudson also seemed to be having a bad time of it. Tom was concerned but decided to give it a day before bothering the veterinarian, and so left Hudson at home.

He walked briskly along the trail all the way to Division Avenue, where the AmeriCo Big Buys store anchored a shopping mall whose resident businesses struggled at various stages of impending failure. This was where Tom got his prescriptions filled. Whenever Tom entered the store, it was cool and alive with people, all looking for food or consumer items that either would or wouldn't kill them. Tom liked the contrast between human chaos and the linear aisles of packaged food, light bulbs, batteries, microbrewed beer, and kitty litter.

Making his way carefully through the parking lot, Old Tom avoided cars that backed out suddenly or honked their horns in annoyance about someone daring to get in their way. He was about to cross the pull-in lane where the grocery bag boys shifted packages from carts to SUVs, while impatient soccer moms tapped their wedding rings against their steering wheels, when Old Major Tom Keenan, looking into the bright glare of the summer sun, thought he saw such a mom in the driver's seat of a Toyota Tundra with two big kids in the back wiggling about. He was standing directly in front of the vehicle when he realized, with growing horror, that the woman was not young but old and wore a confused, frightened expression, and that the two big kids in the back were actually a pair of Rottweilers.

Bea Friday had arrived, like a dark angel in a black truck with a four-speed automatic transmission and tires the size of hot tubs.

It wasn't her intention, actually, to do any damage, but as soon as Bea saw Old Tom, she was so startled that she stepped on the accelerator pedal, making the Tundra pitch forward. The impact knocked Tom to the ground—all of this in slow-motion from Tom's perspective—and the truck ran over Tom's lower legs with the front wheels.

It was known, at least around Dandelion Court, that Bea Friday was a gentle soul who loved books, knitting, and gardening.

But when someone nearby screamed, it so terrified Bea that she cranked the wheel, pushed the transmission into reverse, and ran the wheels across Tom's body for the second time, this time hitting different parts of the body. Tom's struggling and movement stopped.

The item in the suburban edition of the city paper that evening noted that "Mr. Keenan sustained serious head and lower-body injuries and is in critical condition."

Actually, the news was not up to date. By the time Tom arrived in the emergency vehicle at Northfield Central, it was indeed a fact that Tom was dead.

For as long as Dandelion Court has been Dandelion Court, there had never been a tragedy, nor a mystery, so curious and unsettling. An investigation into Tom's death took place, but as yet no one has been able to explain Bea Friday's successful escape from her son's house, or how she found Gus and Rose, the two Rottweilers, nor could anyone guess how she managed, in her state of confusion, to find the AmeriCo Big Buys store on Division Avenue, or if she was even intending to reach that destination.

And, of course, Bea herself couldn't remember anything about it at all.

15.

Tom Keenan saw no bright corridor of light inviting him into the womb of the Universe. Nor did he feel torn between life and death, as if he had a say in the matter at this point.

Instead, Tom found himself walking down the park trail at about three in the afternoon. Must've been early September, judging by the angle of the sun's rays, visible to him as columns of light piercing through the forest canopy.

Far from anticipating eternity, Old Tom looked forward to the cold beer waiting in the fridge back at his house.

Walking in and out of shadows—really walking, not floating,

as some might imagine the experience—Tom tried to keep his eyes open. The packed-gravel trail was the color of a desert-bleached bone, impossibly bright.

Tom forgot about the beer, then forgot about forgetting, and, finally, what had been was no more.

Just like that.

16.

Mike Keenan, Tom's only known immediate family, attended to the business administration of Tom's death. Old Major Tom's wish was to be cremated and his remains composted in the living forest soil in some quiet and remote corner of the park. No record exists as to the carrying out of the dispersal of Tom's ashes.

No church service stirred the souls of the living, so far as anyone remembers. Instead, there was a wake at Neighbor Jack's house. Mike Keenan, whose two boys and wife were present, as the reason for their discomfort was now gone, gave a short oration touting his deceased brother's finer qualities, avoiding for the most part the darkness of Tom's struggle with depression.

"Tom had his demons," Mike said, and left it at that.

Tom had prepared a single page of directives pertaining to the distribution of property. The will indicated that the ownership of the house revert solely to Diana, who, divorced from Tim, lived there alone contentedly for many years, until she married a third husband. They eventually sold the house at 2214 Dandelion Court and moved counterclockwise around the beltway to the Walnut Creek Estates, a gated community through which no creek flowed and no walnut trees grew.

As these things go, Old Major Tom Keenan probably would have been satisfied. Even happy.

17.

The creek running through the park near Dandelion Court had once been nearly dead. Railroad construction, swamp reclamation, and dumped sawmill wastes, as well as open latrines dug by workers and then abandoned as they filled up with bodily wastes, all put a strain on the creek's very survival. Today it is part of a beautiful, naturalized tree-shaded environment. The clean flow of water through a suburban vastness that included the Dandelion neighborhood is a source of respite and regeneration every week for hundreds of people. And their dogs.

On a recent walk the summer following Old Major Tom's unfortunate death in the parking lot of AmeriCo Big Buys, which was now a Blue Danube Superstore, Neighbor Jack held two dog leashes, at the end of which Shelley and Hudson dawdled, smelling everything, looking like a comedy team, and eliciting smiles from everyone who passed them on the trail.

Jack wondered if, in his last moments, Old Major Tom had worried who would take care of Hudson if Tom died first. As if, thought Neighbor Jack, there had ever been any question.

It was the first day in almost a year that Jack had walked the trail. He thought even Old Major Tom Keenan would have been happy on such a day.

Jack took the dogs to his favorite spot, just off a side-trail that ended at a curve in the creek where the water was deep enough for kids in their teens and early twenties to jump or dive from cliffs thirty feet from the pool below the falls. It was one of those magical days and places that reminded Jack of being young, full of youthful desperation and blind courage. He watched one boy dive, a beautiful swanlike floating descent into the deep blue water. How were these kids going to cope with the world being handed them like so much nuclear waste?

Neighbor Jack recalled what Old Major Tom Keenan had said that day only sometime last year. That it seemed like Nature was turning against us. Jack watched the boy disappear into the water with hardly a splash and wondered if he would ever surface.

18.

Thirty years hence, we might like to think, Dandelion Court will have reverted to its original undeveloped condition, a swampy, mosquito-infested parcel of raw acreage, which, like our whole crumbling civilization, was searching for the nearest exit door.

In fact, though, it continues, with new mortgages, fresh coats of paint on the houses, hydrogen-powered cars in the garages, and younger families with children and dogs and cats and automated lawn sprinklers on solar-powered timers and smart windows that keep the heat out in summer and the warmth in during winter.

Just down the path, there is still a cemetery with a few recently occupied graves whose headstones will be puzzled over by the good people of the Dandelion neighborhood, if they can find the time during their busy lives to make such journeys.

Thus do we find Neighbor Jack, at age 88, still walking, though now stiff-legged, down the parkland path, so alone since Glynda died five years ago. Major Tom had actually left this life thirty years ago to the day. That was the way things happened in Dandelion Court, right to the day.

Walking slowly towards the cemetery, Neighbor Jack affirms to himself that he is at least still in his own house, like a dinosaur reluctant to be considered extinct. The only way they will get him to leave, Neighbor Jack believes, will be by picking up his body from wherever he leaves it that one last time.

Progress

If you'd seen Charlie Oliphant after he'd spent that time in the county jail down in Roseburg, you might have gotten the feeling that in a lot of ways he'd sort of died. I saw him myself not too long ago back in Yoncalla where he has his ranch. It was just a short visit I almost wish I hadn't made. Charlie's eyes have sort of dipped back into his head a bit and he's real quiet. Can't talk or won't.

The same with Mike. Mike went sour on country life and when he got out of jail he drove his pick-up farther south, down to L.A., I guess. So far as I know he's back to street-corner folk music and starvation. It's too bad, because people really admired him for sticking his neck out along with Charlie Oliphant on that interstate business. But he's gone. No use talking.

As for Charlie, well, the old man mostly wanders around his place and pitches rocks at the tired, half-starved cattle he hasn't bothered to feed lately. Charlie's music has dried up and blown away.

Kind of hard knowing where to begin. I suppose the Corral Tavern down in Yoncalla would be as good a place as any. It was getting pretty late there as Judy and I leaned our elbows on the polished hardwood bar and drank some more of the free wine that Mick Disheroon, the fellow who owned the Corral, had broken out of his store-room in honor of Charlie Oliphant. This isn't really where it started but it all pretty much came to a head here. Kind of like a minor convulsion.

But you wouldn't know that by looking. There was Mike on the stage up front, hugging his battered guitar while he waited for Charlie Oliphant to snake his way through the crowd. With one hand Charlie waved his fiddle up above his head like he was swimming across a lake, and with the other he wielded the bow like a horsehair rapier. The crowd grudged him an aisle; it was as if Charlie were parting waters.

Judy and I stood down at the end of the bar sipping Gallo Burgundy from Styrofoam cups. We were just watching and enjoying, trying not to think of what had happened. Of what might happen yet. We'd been staying the summer with Mike in his little shack on the edge of Charlie Oliphant's land, just outside of Yoncalla. He had the shack, a worn-out Ford pick-up truck, and a small garden where he grew his own vegetables. Not much else. Judy had brought a few things from Seattle when we came down by Greyhound in early June: her thick Persian rug, a couple Vermeer prints she'd bought in Europe the summer before, the battered copper teapot from the little Italian delicatessen in the Pike Street Market. Just a few things, but they helped make the shack seem homey.

As I watched Mike up there on the makeshift plywood stage, I wondered how he could stay so placid. The highway police were probably on their way right now. Mike knew that well enough; he'd called them. But maybe that was all part of the act—part of the protest. A small perfecting touch, perhaps. Mike savored purity.

"If Charlie makes it up here," Mike announced to the crowd, "We're going to play the Black Mountain Rag." The edge in his voice implied more: For Christ's sake, give the old man room.

Mike was tall with the body and features of an impassive hardwood lamp-post. He'd always looked like that. The Mike I'd known in high school three or four years ago in Seattle would have been interchangeable, on the outside at least, with this one. About the only new thing was the dung-colored cowboy hat he wore nowadays. It was in roughly the same stage of dissipation as his guitar. Mike's jacket was some retired army rag he'd picked up in a First Avenue surplus store last winter back in Seattle. That was when he was giving sidewalk performances on Pike Street and passing a hat around for contributions. I guess he pretty near starved in Seattle and it was just chance that I happened to be in the Market one day when he was playing. He saw me when he was in the middle of a Woody Guthrie talkin' blues and even though we recognized each other right off, he kept going until it was done. I went over to him, not him to me, and I invited him up to Judy's and my apartment. He stayed for about three months, until the weather got better, then left for Oregon.

Mick Disheroon's tavern was full-up. Hardly room to breathe. I'd been inside only once before, with Mike about a month ago. We'd come in for a couple of beers and within five minutes some rancher dude from Drain wanted to pick a fight. No provocation. He was simply a bastard. Big burly guy with tufts of thick black hair on the backs of his hands. Mike and I left, fast. We'd heard stories about people getting busted up and tossed through windows in that place. There never had to be a reason, either; the Corral was simply that kind of tavern.

Now, though, it seemed a different place. The longhairs from Moo Farm commune mixed freely with the local ranchers, and everyone appeared to be enjoying himself. They were all behind Mike and Charlie on the interstate affair, so they said, even the locals who a couple weeks ago had thought of Mike as just another freak come to sponge off the land and the community and Charlie Oliphant. It gave me a little bit of hope that all these people could co-exist peacefully, at least for one night. They'd just needed a common cause, like the one Mike and Charlie had provided. Not really provided, but brought into the open and acted upon.

Charlie finally broke wheezing and panting through the front line and stepped onto the platform where Mike was waiting. Mike cradled his guitar, a Martin, old and mellowed like aged cheese.

"Make it smoke, Charlie!" somebody yelled. Laughter.
But even before the laughter had died out, the old man's fiddle was whining out the first notes of the rag, impatiently scratching at the upper reaches of the e-string as Mike began digging into the bass notes with deep, easy strokes. Except for an occasional glance at the movement of Mike's hands, Charlie kept his eyes on the neck of the fiddle. The toes of his right foot made the faintest tapping motions, vaguely suggesting rhythm.

I'd liked Charlie from the first. He reminded me some of Judy's grandfather Hollis, a seventy-two-year-old man who operated a grain elevator on the Mississippi River back in Minnesota.

Both old timers, both hanging on to life.

Charlie treated Judy kind of like a daughter, or a granddaughter, calling her Sugarplum and doing crazy nice things like buying her a pretty new mail-order dress out of the Sears catalog, and baking her a rhubarb pie on her birthday.

"Come on down," Mike had written us in June when we were finishing up the spring quarter at the university. "There's this old guy who has some land with a shack he's letting me stay in. Room enough for all of us if you feel like getting out of the city."

We had. The day after Judy's last final we took a Greyhound south to Yoncalla where Mike met us at the bus stop, just a wide spot in front of the grocery store. He smiled a greeting as we climbed down. His face and neck were tanned copper-brown; he looked healthier than I'd ever seen him.

After a week or so of sleeping late and wandering around the country roads and watching the sun climb across the sky and sink lazily in the afternoons, I found a job in the veneer plant just outside of town. Judy drove me to work every morning in Mike's old pick-up and I spent the day doing heavy shit-work cleaning up and that sort of thing. It was all right. It made enough money so that we could buy what little we needed and I was able to save a little to put toward school next fall. There was always that.

Judy and I had promised ourselves we'd go back to school after summer was over, no matter how much we liked country living. Mike had said he wasn't sure what he'd do. He was helping work Charlie's ranch but he didn't get paid or anything.

He and Charlie let their tune run for close to ten minutes. By the end of Charlie's first break, the whole tavern was rattling and shaking like loose freight. I'd heard the song a hundred times but I could still enjoy the way it wandered up and down and twisted around like a crooked old tree or a path winding through some crazy forest.

Charlie would saw out an incredible break that you'd think had to be the end of the song because nothing could top it, but then Mike would take off flying on his Martin, fingers blurring, cross-picking and choking and sliding high while Charlie droned a smooth backup. They didn't really try to out-do each other, though. They just loved the music and wanted everyone else to love it.

Finally old Charlie traded Mike a look, and they both moved high on the necks and reeled out a tight, syncopated variation that floated in the clouds for a short minute and then dropped like a bucket of water back to earth. The rag was finished.

I jerked my mind back into context as Judy poured Gallo into the Styrofoam cups. Things would start happening pretty soon. Stuff that depressed me to think about. I smelled grass and wondered if the ranchers got off on having dope floating around inside their tavern. Charlie waved off cries for an encore with criss-cross slicing motions of his bow. He swished his hand in front of his face as though he were brushing flies off and pinched his nose up closer to his eyes in a distasteful squint.

The place roared laughter. Charlie began fencing his way back in the same direction he'd come, turning once to give a little nod to Mike who was left standing alone on the make-shift stage, half-leaning over his Martin guitar.

Then the old man was gone. He seemed to have been re-absorbed into the shuffling sea of bodies.

"Do you still have the keys to the pick-up?" I asked Judy.

"In here," Judy said dangling the leather pouch she kept her money and things in. I was for some reason caught up in details. If Mike was arrested, someone would have to take the truck. Judy, probably. I had this feeling I might end up going to Roseburg before the night was over. I'd have to find out about posting bail, getting a lawyer, all the legal hassles.

"Hang onto them," I said.

Judy smiled, tired. She has brown, stringy hair, not real pretty hair, and some loose strands were hanging in her face. She brushed them back.

I spent a few minutes talking to Mick Disheroon about nothing in particular. Mick looked chipper and I felt dull and slow beside him. As he gabbed I thought how the whole evening had swept right along up to Charlie's performance but now that it was over everyone just seemed to want to rock a little on his heels and yawn down another glass of free wine. I felt the same.

A guitar started up somewhere. Not Mike's. This was mellower. I turned and saw that a guy from one of the communes in the hills east of Yoncalla had climbed onto the stage with his nylon-string guitar. He picked delicately at the melody of "East Virginia," then began to sing in a high, nice-sounding voice. Mike stood back and out of his way, listening politely. No one else paid much attention. I thought it was fine music but couldn't hear much of it. Mainly just the voice. It was like a choirboy's and so it rang out above the racket.

Mike listened for a minute and then stepped down from the stage. He bedded his Martin in the battered hard shell case that leaned open against the wall. Straightening, he craned his neck looking around for Charlie. He spotted Judy and me, flickered a smile and came over to the bar.

"It was nice," Judy said as Mike poured himself an old marmalade jar full of Gallo. "Real nice. I liked the last part, the duet. You can teach me the guitar half any time."

Mike grinned. "Oh, nothing to teach, really. You just sort of fake it."

I glanced at Judy as we all laughed and I tried to imagine her a country girl, like when she'd lived with an aunt and uncle outside Duluth. Maybe she would be again. Her face had always seemed to me in some manner a country face: deeply tanned, rather long and drawn, big brown eyes full of patience. The bright cotton Sears dress Charlie had bought for her kind of swirled in careless rumples around her body and made her seem perfectly at ease, as if she were sitting in the sunlit kitchen of an old farmhouse sipping coffee and contemplating the agenda of morning chores. The dress wasn't a real great fit but neither of us cared because it was worth it just to see Charlie's wrinkled face light up when he saw her in it.

"Disappeared. I lost sight of him."

We all swung our heads around and tried to spot the old man's silver-white hair. That was when Ed Cauley came up and patted Judy on the ass. Ed was one of the lead men down at the veneer plant and was about as big as two of me. He always called me Sonny, which grated a little. That time Mike and I had been in the Corral for a beer I'd seen Ed hunched over a half-empty glass looking drunk and belligerent as hell. When the rancher from Drain wanted to pick a fight, Ed just sort of grinned over at us and took a swallow of beer, waiting to be amused. I didn't much like him. He was one of those small town "characters" who always sounds real interesting to talk about but when you meet them and have to deal with them it's suddenly a different story.

Ed greeted Mike with a slap on the back.

"Seventy miles of traffic backed up both ways," he said noisily. He breathed wine into Mike's face. Judy set her wine on the bar and sort of rotated around to the other side of me so that I separated her from Ed. "Heard it on the radio 'safternoon. Highway patrol. Bet they're mad as hell."

The new freeway, new since fall, flowed glacier-like down through the wooded hills below Cottage Grove, emptied out flat by Drain, and bowed in a fish-backed hump around Charlie Oliphant's alfalfa. Alfalfa grew on one side, wheat on the other, the east side; it was all one piece before the freeway. Now, though, there's six lanes of concrete between fields and that is why Charlie and Mike spent time in jail. That's where it started.

"A hundred forty miles of hot-headed tourists strung out like a snake in the sun," Ed bellowed, his face screwed into a crooked smile.

It was funny, now, that people like Ed Cauley, people who didn't farm or ranch or have some stake in the land, weren't as sympathetic with Charlie and Mike about what the two of them had done. They couldn't really understand what it meant to have a freeway running straight down the center of your spread so that you couldn't even reach the far side when it came time to harvest your wheat. They thought that if the highway commissioned all those bigshot engineers who said that a freeway had to go in such-and-such a place, well, that's all there was to it. Ed Cauley was like that.

His smile poked fun at Mike's predicament, saying something like: "Now what earthly good did all this good do you, boy? All you got for yourself is a lot of trouble."

Mike backed away from Ed and mumbled that he had to go piss or something like that. He wandered off. Deprived of a target, Ed turned to me.

"How's it going, Sonny?"

I didn't say anything and finally Ed Cauley just sort of snorted and huffed off.

The folk singer up on the stage had finished "East Virginia" and was starting in on "Barbara Allen" but he gave up after the first verse. Too much noise. He hopped down and went to sit at the other end of the bar where he began drinking wine and smoking cigarettes. I thought I'd seen him before in some other context. Maybe Seattle. Maybe he'd gone to the university.

Someone fed money to the jukebox and Johnny Cash came on with "Ring of Fire." The music was turned up so loud I could feel the vibration in the floor. Then Mike returned and said he'd found Charlie.

"Over there." Mike nodded toward the rear of the tavern. He pushed our way through the crowd.

Charlie was propped stiffly in a straight-backed chair that leaned against the fake oak-paneled wall. His fiddle rested face down across his lap and he spread his hands over its gently curving, fawn-colored spine. Slanted shadows from the front of the tavern spread back and divided the old man's face into diagonal bars.

"They'll come," Charlie said as though he were predicting rain. "Pretty soon now, I guess."

Mike nudged his shoulders a little higher in what might have been a shrug, then glanced around behind him at the dance floor. It was packed. I could feel the heat that oozed from all those bodies. All those bodies which had become, in a couple short months, neighbors of ours. More or less. Some of them were starting to sway and boogie to the flashy clang of electric country-rock that spurted unevenly from the jukebox. With his fingertips Charlie began tapping a patient rhythm of his own on the back of the fiddle.

"How you doing, Sugarplum?" he said smiling to Judy. "Jesus but you're pretty tonight." His pale green eyes swept up and down her body.

"Thanks, Charlie. It's this dress."

Charlie peshawed that with a half-disgusted snort.

"Like hell." He looked at her so keenly I think Judy might have been a little embarrassed. Hell of an old guy. Still hanging onto life.

"Look," Mike said, turning back to Charlie, "we can leave if we want; go back to the place and wait for them there. I don't much like it here either."

"Naw," Charlie growled. "Don't want to go just now. Stick around, see what happens."

Mike let a thin smile rise. I knew enough about him to realize that he wasn't about to leave, not now. This whole interstate fiasco had meant a lot to him and he'd carry it through to the inevitable conclusion: police, court, jail. It meant a lot to Charlie too, but in a different way. For Charlie it was a kind of hand-to-hand combat with the people who built the freeway down the center of his land. He knew who the bad guys were, and his actions had been aimed specifically at them. With Mike, though, it wasn't quite the same. Mike's targets weren't so concrete.

His bad guy was an economic power structure so big and complex that you couldn't see where it started and where it ended. All you could see or feel was that certain part that came down on your own little microcosm.

"Okay," Mike said, "we'll wait here."

We grabbed three empty wooden crates that lay in a clutter of empty bottles and dusty assorted junk a few feet away and shoved them up against the wall next to Charlie. From there we had a fairly clear view of the front door.

"Like a damn party," Charlie grumbled, gazing at the crowd and working the words in a low tone from one side of his mouth.

He was right. All of a sudden I wondered what all of these people thought they were doing here. It was like a party we had in high school for the basketball team after the last game of the season. The home team lost, but everyone felt we had to go ahead and give the thing anyway.

Slowly Charlie began rocking back and forth in his chair, making it creak. Sometimes we all sat like this on Charlie's front porch. It was especially nice during the summer when the sun began dipping west into afternoon and the little cedar-shingled lean-to roof covering the veranda shaded us from the heat. A breeze usually came up around four o'clock and blew a mowed-grass sweetness in from the fields. We didn't do much talking. Just sat. Charlie maintained the same pose as always, kind of wooden and serene, one foot tapping the rhythm to some lonesome tune that rambled like a lost child through his head. From the porch we could look out on most of his land, out across the alfalfa that spread like a dark, waving lawn, down-sloping, dropping away until the wheat started its rise across the valley. Forty acres of golden wheat, down from the eighty Charlie used to raise before he sold the upper half to a sheep rancher. That piece was worthless to anybody now. Overgrazed. Made Charlie madder than hell to think about the waste.

From the porch we could look out past the graying pine poles supporting the roof to where Charlie's small herd of white-faced cattle gnawed grass in a north pasture. A hundred yards in the other direction, still on Charlie's land, sat the three-room shack where Mike and Judy and I stayed. It squatted beneath an oak. There were a few flowers in the bed that circled around the bottom, and on a plot just north of the shack was the garden that Mike and Judy cared for like a newborn lamb. The place had begun to seem like a home, and I enjoyed sitting on Charlie's porch where I could just gaze over and watch it. The afternoon breezes made the oak leaves rustle above the stone chimney, a sound like water rushing over rocks in the bed of a stream, and Charlie's peaceful rocking punctuated the calm spots with a steady succession of creaking. Good for daydreaming. The pine slats of the old decaying porch groaned a little, just like the chair the old man now sat on inside the Corral.

The noise inside the tavern had risen to a single loud, unfocused din. Streaming long hair waved in dancing swirls to the blaring music, and sculptured Stetsons bobbed severely as though the men underneath them were standing on hot stoves. Mike folded his hands behind his head.

"What a bunch of…" His voice trailed off.

"It's pretty ridiculous," I finished for him. I wasn't sure, though. Maybe it's the way it should have been. The scene in the tavern no longer had anything to do with Charlie or Mike or the interstate or the cops who were on their way from Roseburg. Maybe that was for the best. It had turned into one hell of a party.

Mike just leaned back against the wall and stretched his legs idly in front of him so that he had the air of some cynical store-front loafer ready to spit tobacco. A hundred dancing feet swept the floor like brooms. Then the front door swayed open and the sweeping sound wavered uncertainly for a moment, thinned, and finally evaporated. Only the aimless peal of whiny guitars raged through the tavern. Then, abruptly, even that stopped, as if on cue.

"See? They came, all right," Charlie declared in a slightly drawling tone that might just as well have been used to say, "See? I told you it would rain." Mike nodded, still leaning against the wall. It was as though everything had suddenly been slapped back into sharp perspective. It was all of a sudden clear again where the focus of the evening lay.

A swath cleared through the crowd, laying open a bare stretch of scuffed hardwood floor that led from Sheriff Olmes and two state troopers to the back of the room where we were sitting. I noticed that we were all slouched lazily on our boxes, as if we might be staring out across nothing more than forty acres of alfalfa. I'd been nervous, but now I was just tired.

As the three officers marched self-consciously across the floor, the thought hit me that they might be a little nervous about their own standing. Twinges of uneasiness flickered across their faces. The older of the two troopers had a paunch that sagged some over his belt. I'd seen him before, driving through Yoncalla. Never seen his buddy, a younger guy. Bick Olmes, now, I was surprised to see him tonight. I'd talked to Bick a couple times before and kind of liked him because he seemed good-natured behind those soft red jowls. About as unlikely a candidate for sheriff as I'd ever seen. As he came toward us across the floor, I could see that his cheeks were bruised with a purplish flush, as though he'd just run two miles.

When they stopped in front of us, the troopers stood one or two steps behind Sheriff Olmes with their thumbs hooked identically over the tops of their leather belts. Bick held an official-looking piece of paper. He blinked recognition at us.

"Charlie," he sort of croaked, "there's a warrant out for you. For you and this here fellow," he said with a nod at Mike. I had to smile as Bick fluttered the paper a little bit like he was trying to shake it loose from his fingers. The tavern was quiet as the bottom of a lake.

"What fer." Charlie dropped the words in well-spaced throbs.

"Obstructin' traffic, to begin with," Bick came right back, real professional-sounding.

"Obstructin' what?"

"Traffic, Charlie."

Charlie, without really moving, seemed, to gather himself up and inward like the rising surge of a wave about to crest. "The way I see it," he unwound, "it was tra-ffic obstructin' me."

The first patterings of laughter trickled from Charlie's audience. The troopers darkened. Finally, after an uneasy silence, just as I was beginning to think that the unbelievable might happen—that the whole incident might be passed over as a tremendous prank of some sort—one of the troopers slipped around in front of Bick Olmes and seemed to stage a miniature coup d'etat.

"Okaybudthatsenough," he sputtered. He snatched the paper like he was capturing a flag and stuffed it into his rear pocket. I heard Judy whisper Oh Jesus or something and then the trooper snarled "Sonofabitch" and I knew right then that it wasn't a joke to him.

This was about the point where Charlie rose with his slow, decrepit flourish. I'd seen Charlie Oliphant get up from a chair in that manner only once before, way back in June when I first knew him. Charlie's brother Zeke had come all the way up to Yoncalla to beg eighty dollars because he said he wanted to buy a new sheepdog pup. Hell, Charlie said later, Zeke never owned a sheep in his life. He'd just blow the eighty on a good time. So then when Zeke tried to wring gas money from Charlie for the trip back to Medford the old man just got up out of his rocker on the porch, real slow and easy, and did something, I'm not sure what, but the next thing I knew Zeke was sort of bouncing down the wooden steps with this surprised look on his face like he'd just discovered he had eleven fingers.

So there was Charlie, facing off with the older of the two troopers and looking calm as Sunday morning. Nobody in the tavern except for me and Judy and Mike could really see how he all at once poked the trooper's belly with the tip of his bow; they saw only the quick upjerk of the khaki knee as the trooper grabbed it and casually snapped it into two uneven pieces that dangled from a limp swish of horsehair. The brittle crack of the wood opened a silence like the innards of some deserted farmhouse.

Then, out of the blue:

"Up yours, pig."

There were at least a hundred people in the tavern and ninety-nine of them were looking around to try and figure out who had yelled. I thought to myself, Christ, not now. None of this hate thing to complicate matters. You don't pull university stunts in a crowd full of half-looped rednecks, with a couple of no-nonsense state troopers standing by.

But it was already taking effect. The words fastened in the air and hung. Mike, who had jumped to his feet the instant the bow had been broken, now stood with his knuckles wrapped into a knobbed ball and his eyes focused on the trooper's face. Judy put her hand on his arm and I stood up alongside him.

"Forget it, Mike," I said. "Let's not start anything now." The act of protest had already been completed this afternoon. All this crap was simply undercutting its beauty and effectiveness.

"Off you, pig!" the same voice, tight, high-pitched and boyish, rang out, this time louder. It came from the other end of the bar and this time I thought I recognized it: the folk singer from earlier in the evening. It hit me. I had seen him before: one of the protesters who had busted into my political science class the previous spring. I'd listened to him accuse the professor of fascism and I'd watched as he toppled the podium to the floor with a sweep of his arm. It seemed like a completely pointless gesture.

"Come on, everybody," he urged. "Off-the-pig, off-the-pig, off-the-pig…"

The trooper and Mike still glared at each other. The trooper's head twitched as if it wanted to fly off into space all by itself and come crashing down like a block of stone on the guy who was yelling. Nobody joined in the chant. Poor Bick Olmes didn't know what to make of it and his embarrassed flush deepened and fragmented into spots the size of fruit flies.

"Come on! OFF-THE-PIG! OFF-THE-PIG! OFF-THE…"

I heard something like a dull whip-crack and then it was quiet. The trooper's head rolled one-eighty as if he were the one who had been hit and he made a flicking hand motion to his partner. I turned toward where Charlie had been standing all this time but the old man was gone.

The trooper, who still had the ruined bow draped across his outstretched hand, as though offering it to Mike, blew a sharp impatient spray of air through his teeth and nodded over to the back door, which still flapped on its hinges. Charlie must have gone out through it. The second trooper, the younger guy I'd never seen before, now waded into the crowd, which had gathered into a tight ball around some unseen nucleus on the floor. He disappeared except for his hat. It floated on the sea of heads, nodded out of view for a moment, then surfaced again.

Mike took a step backward. He gently shook loose Judy's hand, slid from under my own, which I'd placed on his shoulder both with the idea of calming and restraining, and executed a sort of inverted lunge, which backed him heavily through the door Charlie had gone out of. A few ranchers and some of the commune people were by now gathering around Bick Olmes asking what the hell was going on, was Ed Cauley going to jail too for busting the kid's jaw, and where in Sam Hill was Charlie Oliphant. Bick looked astonished. I told Judy to go out the front way and start the truck up because no matter what happened we were leaving pretty soon and then I followed Mike out the back. I pushed through the door and scrambled in the dusty lot between shiny cars parked in a gleaming tangle under the moon. Finally I found him standing quiet as piney woods on a warm day by the side of the highway patrol car. I came up behind him. We could see the interstate off in the distance.

"Oh, just say to hell with all that business inside," I said.

"Yeah… where'd Charlie go?" I shook my head.

"It's getting all fucked up," Mike said. "He should never have done that to Charlie."

"Charlie sort of asked for it. He's no kid. He knew." Mike looked at me like I'd kicked him. I hadn't meant it to sound quite so blunt.

"He'll show up," I said quickly, trying to erase the bruise. "Probably just went to take a piss." Mike didn't laugh. I tried but couldn't. Charlie hadn't gone to take any piss.

We watched silently as the endless lights slid through darkness on the interstate, curving easily around Charlie's alfalfa a little farther south and disappearing into mere flickers of red in the distance. More lights, white ones, reversed the flow as the cars and trucks behind them moved north from Sutherlin and Roseburg.

I hadn't even known that Charlie and Mike had planned to do it until after they'd gone ahead. I was at work when it happened. Maybe Judy knew. I'm not sure. When I got home around five-thirty I found Mike and Charlie sitting on the porch grinning like two kids who'd just looted a candy store. The alfalfa that spread down in front of Charlie's house waved gently in the afternoon breeze and farther below, from the freeway, came an incredible symphony of honking cars and trucks.

I heard Judy start the pick-up out front, but I kept staring at the flares that glowed brightly on the curve, the curve where the thing now ending had begun. I guessed they were still cleaning up the mess. I could imagine the confused shadows the phosphorous warning flares would make of the mangled guard rails and twisted cyclone fencing that had been ripped loose and strewn about in mutilated jumbles this afternoon when Mike and Charlie had eased the two snorting bulldozers up the embankment and onto the interstate, laying their strings of concrete-chewing harrows and disc-plows in a neat east-west line across eight lanes. It must have been a sight.

Both Mike and I jerked around as the tavern door creaked open. The first trooper, the one who had snapped Charlie's bow in half, came outside nudging Ed Cauley. Ed kept inching forward in short, tangled lunges. The trooper flicked his head toward the patrol car and Mike climbed quietly into the back seat.

"Who are you?" he asked, nodding at me. His voice sounded tired.

"Friend. We board together."

"You come, too," the trooper said, then added, and I almost sympathized with him: "This is one goddamn mess."

I climbed in and the trooper guided Ed Cauley in beside me. Ed groaned for a minute about how he'd bruised his fist on the kid's jaw. Then he yawned once and passed out. His head was thrown back so that the skin over the front of his neck stretched taut, making his Adam's apple protrude enormously like a barren, lumpy mountain.

The state trooper slammed the door, disappeared into the bar again, and came back out followed by his partner and Bick Olmes. The three of them squeezed uncomfortably into the front seat and the car jumped forward.

"Stop here for a minute, will you?" I said when we'd gone around to the front. Judy sat in the idling pick-up.

"Who's that?"

"My wife." That simplified matters.

Judy stuck her head out of the cab window and I had to lean across the front seat and use that window because the back one didn't open.

"Wait around for Charlie a few minutes," I said. "If he shows up, take him home. If he doesn't, go home yourself. See you in the morning."

I smiled, telling myself I would by God see her in the morning.

"I guess I have to go to Roseburg." I felt lousy after saying that. I didn't want much to go to Roseburg, and the prospect depressed me. The trooper whose window I was leaning from nudged me back into my seat beside Ed Cauley. I peered through the window and held my hand flat against the safety glass, a kind of parting wave. I noticed that Judy was sitting in the funniest way. She had her chin propped between the V of her thumb and forefinger and she seemed to be thinking about some distant land. I wondered what was going through her head. I wondered if she'd known about the whole plan and just didn't tell me. She and Mike spent days together on the farm so they must have talked a lot. I'd never thought much about that before.

Finally she smiled, sort of empty and sad, and we screeched off, gravel skittering from under the wheels of the patrol car.

We drove about a quarter mile.

The trooper pumped the brakes and stopped twenty yards

short of the spot where Charlie Oliphant stood frozen in the center of the road like a mesmerized rabbit caught in the over-exposed glare of headlights. He was without his fiddle, and his blue denim shirt had been uprooted from his pants and torn into ragged, flag-like morsels as though he had tunneled through a patch of blackberry brambles. His neck craned forward and his face shaped itself around a bent, off-center grin. His head appeared somehow crooked in relation to the rest of his body, and he began making limp, disjointed waving motions with his arms that made it seem on the one hand as if he were flagging a ride, and on the other as if, perhaps, all his bones were broken.

Mason Dixon

"Shush," my mom said gently to me. "Just shush."

I stopped crying and looked at Mom again. She was so fragile, yet her face still showed such wonder and love. We looked into each others' eyes for a moment, just looked.

Even though I didn't know Death by name, I knew, suddenly and irrefutably, that Mom was going to die. Maybe not this month or even this year or the next. It wasn't the schedule, it was the raw fact. I knew it to be true: Someday, Mom would be gone and I will still be here.

I think I might have just had my third birthday.

Valerie
Many things I still do not understand. Such as, why have I chosen this journey back to Arkansas? Did I think there would be some magical closure with the past? I never wondered about "why" I was given this illness, because it doesn't make any more sense than it does to see otherwise healthy young people dying of cancer or in car accidents while I muddle on, slowly but progressively losing my grip.

Shush asks me where the Mason-Dixon Line is located. I'm not sure why the interest, but I always thought it had something to do with free versus slave states during the time before the Civil War. Wherever it may lie, I must have crossed without realizing it when I came south from Duluth to find a warmer climate.

Was my first lover's name really Mason Dixon? With him, did I cross a line into a new frontier? A place where a pregnant woman is sitting in an abortion clinic, while outside, protesters shout ugly, violent things and tell me I am a murderer?

It was not Mason (if that was his name), who was left to work out the deal with God and the being inside me. Yes or no? I cried and said how sorry I was, that this was a terrible time for me to have a child. I felt selfish and contemptible.

Several years later, my then-new husband Richard and I brought into our life a different child. A beautiful daughter Richard and I have called Shush, because she is like the calming sound of a breeze passing through green leaves at the height of summer. Shush, who watches over me so carefully, not making it too obvious that she is the one who is taking care of me.

Shush

Mom's em-ess is coming back.

I remembered *it*, the way it made her look, how her feet seemed as if they were being moved by someone else in directions she didn't understand. She was more frequently dropping things, sometimes a favorite ceramic mug, sometimes the piece of chicken she was trying to place in the pan on the stove. How tired she always was.

When Mom gave us the news, I already had figured out that she was relapsing. Life slowed down, like it does when things don't go well. Today, time is creeping by so slowly, I just want to scream. Why is it that the best things vanish in a second, like a piece of chocolate cake, or a moment out in the sun when it's been cloudy and raining all day, or opening your Big Present at Christmas? But when you're watching your pet rat die or somebody is saying why they don't like you, that can darken your mood for a long time, maybe your whole life. I'm hardly an expert. I'm just beginning my journey.

Mom told me that pain is unavoidable but suffering is our choice.

She has been in remission and relapse a few times. The relapses hit harder soon after I was born. The em-ess is a tough customer, she says, and when it goes into remission, she feels good. Then suddenly it comes back and tries to swallow her up.

I am ten, nearly eleven. Although Mom is careful in talking to me about this, she did say to a friend once, and I overheard, that she felt better than she had in years during her second and third trimesters. Her em-ess symptoms almost disappeared, then she relapsed big-time a month after my delivery (more on that later). When I asked her if it was my fault she was sick again, she looked at me and cried. "Oh, no," she said with tears tracking down her cheeks. "You are my forever treasure." And she got down on her knees on the kitchen floor and we hugged. I hugged her hard so she would be okay.

Though I believed what she said, there lingered in my mind an almost imperceptible speck of doubt and complicity.

My dad sometimes calls me Eggy because, he says, I'm so smart. But I'm not so smart that I can do much to help Mom besides not giving her too much of my preadolescent grief. In remission, Mom is able to lead a pretty normal life, except for occasional migraines. She works part-time as a paralegal at a downtown personal injury law partnership, takes good care of herself by exercising and doing yoga and tai chi, and gets plenty of rest as well as walks as much as she can. And she is generally hopeful.

When her sickness returned this time, she really got mad at it, furious at the em-ess. She yells into a pillow on a regular basis. I don't know if it helps.

When I came into the world, obviously without a clue about the entropic potential within my Mom's brain, I had a precocious appetite for speed. As my mom would later describe my birth to anyone and everyone, I wasn't really born, I was fired from a cannon—Mom being the cannon—and landed over in the next county. This is partially accurate. We lived in Atlanta, Georgia, which is in Fulton County, but the hospital where I was delivered from the warm darkness of my mom's womb was in Douglasville, fifty miles west of Atlanta in Douglas County, where there was a birthing facility and midwives were part of the medical team.

Mom told me one day when it was just her and me in the house, a bad em-ess day for Mom, and Dad was away on a business trip, that when she was young (she didn't say how young but I think she meant my age) her greatest ambition was to join the circus. Not just in a kind of "this is what I want to do today" way. She told me about the books she had read about the circus, its history, its heroes and villains, the freak shows, the animal abuse, the sleaziness and the glamour, the horrible injuries and even deaths. She talked wistfully, as if she had been there two thousand years ago in Rome for the Circus Maximus, witnessing firsthand the thrilling and deadly chariot races with huge crowds of blood-lusting spectators, sort of like NASCAR races, Mom said. Which I could relate to, as I admit to having a crush on that year's Sprint Cup winner Jimmie Johnson. I thought he was gorgeous.

Then just as unexpectedly as Mom had started telling me about these amazing times and people, something inside her flicked off. I didn't want to let the moment go, so I asked if she ever did join the circus.

"Of course not," she said, with a laugh that made my question feel stupid. I didn't feel like asking any more questions right then. But I saved one for later.

Aunt Debbie

I had to work hard to bring my son Donald into the world and claim him as mine.

Knowing that he had part of a twenty-first chromosome in his DNA didn't make it any easier. Neither did Donald's father.

Sometimes, I think, a person believes she can change who she is in order to make a positive impression on another person. Like she wants a man to think she's openhearted and clever, or some such nonsense, when actually she tends in everyday life to be introverted and rather dull.

That was my big mistake when I started dating Sam. I told him about the meditation retreats I'd gone to, the plays and movies I'd seen, the books I read. And I think I came across as intelligent, independent, and available.

Dishonesty isn't exactly the intention, but because people are—all right, I am—so desperately alone, I would have done anything to find someone who respected and loved me, kept me warm on a cold night, somebody who could help me get through difficult times.

Me and Sam got married about the same time we got pregnant. In fact, I am certain it was the day before we exchanged rings that Donald was conceived. At Sam's condo, we had sex that was earthy and dirty and wonderfully uninhibited. Many squeals and aaahhhs. Father, forgive me.

I grew up Catholic and always assumed a big church wedding to accompany the shame of premarital sex, but ours was more of an efficiency ceremony at a McChapel. Vows, rings, done. Next?

Our marriage was Sam's second, my first. He had two sons, twelve and fifteen, who lived with their mom. In courting me, Sam said all the right things about "blending" families, the latest parenting philosophies, and the importance of having a father in the home. I was such a sucker, I swallowed the bait, hook, line, and sinker.

Looking back, I understand, I think, why Sam did not want another child. He had already failed one family, so why set himself up for another fall? Out of the blue, he insisted on an amniocentesis test, and we learned that the fetus was a boy and that he had part of an extra twenty-first chromosome. Sam's response was to tell me to get an abortion. He wasn't going to bring, as he said, another goddamn demented expensive high-tech-dependent kid into the world. Driving back to Sam's condo, he made it clear what he expected me to do.

"Nobody's taking this baby from me!" I said with a growl of rage that shocked both of us but felt good and right. "We are going to keep this child. It … is … my … decision!" Shouting at each other in the car, I realized this was the end of the road for me and Sam. As if repeating a scene he had watched in a movie, Sam said, "If it's your decision and that's the way you feel about it, then I'm outta here."

And he was.

There were a few half-hearted attempts to pretend it would still work, but as communication between us never again de-escalated from the level of a screaming match whenever we were together, it seemed as if Sam actually became another person. How could I have missed the nose hairs, his creased, unhappy forehead, his squat posture, his bad breath, his naturally greasy hair?

As I entered my third trimester, my sister Valerie called me and announced the happy news that she was pregnant, and was just letting family know for now. She and her husband Richard were thrilled. They took all the prenatal classes that I couldn't afford or get to, and they read books on being the parents of a newborn. I had glanced at a couple free brochures from my public health nurse's office.

We had both lived in Atlanta since we'd left home in Duluth, Minnesota, Val meeting and marrying Richard, getting a good job in Buckhead, and moving into a nice old house on Candler Park, while I blew off a college education I could have ridden out as a shot-putter on an 80-percent athletic scholarship to the University of Georgia, over in Athens.

When it came, my labor with Donald was jarring and agonizing. My water had broken, and Donald was inside me bashing his head and limbs against my unpadded uterus. I thought I was strong. What a joke. And I was alone, except for the doctor and nurses. My suffering did not seem to impress them. Worse, Val had the flu and was unable to help me get through the birth. I begged pathetically for an epidural because it felt like my hip bones were being spread apart by an expanding spacer and would soon just snap apart.

When Donald finally appeared, however, it was all worth it. He looked so perfect, so beautiful, and I loved him and knew I would always love him.

Donald was all I had. When Sam was in the picture during our pregnancy before the amniocentesis, he insisted I stay at home and not work, so I took a leave of absence from Target and it turned out that I exceeded the family leave allowance and had in fact been fired.

I quickly learned about Medicaid, unemployment insurance (a person I knew in Human Resources at Target had me reclassified as laid off), food stamps, Section 8 housing, food banks, low-income health care, and hunger. Unable to afford the apartment for more then a couple of months, Donald and I struggled in a transitional women's shelter that allowed children. I was too proud to accept, for a while, at least, Val's offer to move in with them.

Sam moved to Chicago when Donald was eight months old. He never paid a penny for child support or alimony, and he wouldn't divorce me, why I am not sure. With the little money left from when I briefly had access to Sam's bank account, I paid first and last month plus deposit on a one-bedroom in southwest Atlanta. Our neighbors on one side were drug dealers. I was too scared, once I knew that, to do or say anything about it. I wondered if this is what my life would be, stuck with a child in a tenement apartment complex controlled by drug dealers.

On the other side lived, by herself, an eighty-one-year-old African-American great-grandmother of fourteen named Mrs. Pearl. We didn't become close, but she told me all about her life, though she didn't ask me any questions, as though she could see my life perfectly by just looking at me.

One morning, as we had coffee together following a terrifying night of gunshots, profanity, and police cars with their hypnotic light patterns flashing against our window shades, Mrs. Pearl looked right into my eyes and said, "Girl, you have to get that poor child and yourself out … of … this … place." Mrs. Pearl then softened slightly. "Don't you have any family, Sweetheart?" Somehow she knew I was too proud for my own good. "You go stay with that family, whomsoever they may be, until you get yourself and that fine boy of yours back on your feet."

I almost cried when she described Donald as a "fine" boy.

Previous to that, no one had really said much about him at all. Or they just noted that "he's a big one."

That afternoon I called Val and told her that Donald and I would come and stay with them at least for a while. We moved in that week. I got my damage deposit back from the apartment manager, with Mrs. Pearl's help. It was all the money I had left.

Between me and Donald, there was so little we owned that I could carry it all in a couple of sturdy black trash can bags. I insisted on taking the Metro to Valerie and Richard's house on Candler Park. Val sighed and agreed.

Donald and I took what had been Richard's den from when he did consulting work, and we rearranged things and brought in a double bed for me and a crib that Val picked up at Goodwill. "Richard doesn't really use the room much any more," Val told me, but I sensed that she was also telling me something else about Richard. I didn't want to know about it, at least not at that moment. "The house is big enough for all of us," Val said with a smile.

Val asked me to come to the birth, which was planned to take place out in Douglasville at a birthing center. I told her I'd think about it. Watching anyone, even my sister, giving birth wasn't high on my list just then.

Shush

My favorite song when I was growing up in Atlanta, Georgia, was the version of "Freight Train" played and sung by Elizabeth Cotton, a dark-skinned, wrinkly-faced old woman who played a right-hander's guitar left-handed, so that the thumb on her picking hand was striking the treble strings. Maybe that's what gave the song its haunting quality. I wanted to be the person I imagined in the lyrics. Mom had an old scratchy Folkways vinyl record from the Newport Folk Festival in 1969 with Libby Cotton performing, and I listened to that album a lot. The line about "going so fast" sounded like my life's theme. The thing I didn't know, hadn't figured out, however, was whether I was running towards or away from whatever it was that I was trying to discover or doing my best to forget.

Time was beginning to seem faster again.

"Mom," I asked, "did you have many boyfriends before Dad?" That just came out of the blue one night when Dad was working late. It seemed like he was at work or traveling a lot. It was late afternoon with golden Georgia sky so thick and sumptuous it seemed like back-lit gauze.

Mom and I were sitting on my bed. I'd been reading "Frog and Toad" stories to her, just to practice my reading and pronunciation. I closed the book. Mom looked perturbed at first, but her face softened after a few seconds.

"Only one that mattered," she said quietly.

"Oh, please tell me, Mom. Was he as handsome as Dad?"

"Wel-l-l-l, yes, I think so."

Suddenly a cold feeling passed through me, like a ghost was in the room. Mom said, "Do you want to hear about him?"

I said yes immediately, although I wasn't really sure.

"Okay. Well, you know that your Aunt Debbie and I grew up in Minnesota," she began.

"Of course, Mom," I said impatiently. She looked at me for a few seconds and continued.

"When I was eighteen, I needed to get out of Duluth; I was so sick of rainy 55-degree July days that I could just scream, and I did: screamed and left. In my Dodge Dart, I took the money I'd received from graduation and drove south, toward warmth and sunshine. Veered west, drove into Arkansas and went to Hot Springs. I have no idea why I chose that place to visit. But the weather was nice so I stayed in a hotel for a couple days."

Mom stopped. "Is this really interesting to you?" she asked, and even though so far I was still waiting for something to be interesting, I said yes, I wanted to hear the story.

Mom all of a sudden seemed sad. "I heard there was a circus over in Little Rock, just east of Hot Springs," she continued.

Ah, I thought, the circus.

"I'd never been to a circus, a real circus, and this was a genuine Ringling Brothers Blue Tour show. The real thing, three-ring big top with the flying trapeze, the beautiful horses in the center ring with riders standing on their backs. All the circus you could ask for. Elephants. The human cannonball. I bought a general-admission ticket and started just looking around. Then I saw a man who seemed out of place somehow. He was slowly walking the show horses back to the stable, I guess. He didn't look glamorous or sleazy like the other circus people. He had on a worn cowboy hat and clean work clothes and looked just like a regular person. The next thing happened so fast that I couldn't stop myself. 'Hey,' I shouted across the passageway between tents, 'do you work here?' Stupid question, but that's what came out. He stopped, looked over at me, and said, 'Ah trah,' in just the voice I expected. I felt foolish, of course, but he didn't seem nervous or annoyed or really anything. He just seemed wide open to whatever or whoever came his way. That man became the first love of my life," Mom said. "And yes, he was as handsome as your dad."

"What happened then?" I prodded, secretly hoping she would not tell me.

"I spent the next three weeks with him on the tour. Last show was outside of Atlanta at Stone Mountain. Then he was gone. He just took off once his contract was up, never said good-bye or anything. I stayed in Atlanta and met your dad, but later, after I tried out college for a couple years."

I felt like this was backwards, but I gave Mom a hug, not really understanding the dynamics of the relationship she'd had with the circus guy.

"What was his name?" I asked.

Mom looked at me and seemed to bring her scattered pieces together so that she seemed like Mom again.

"He said his name was Mason Dixon, but I think he just made that up. He broke my heart."

"He didn't ever try to call or send you flowers, or anything?"

Mom hesitated, then said, "He left a gift for me."

But she wouldn't say what it was.

Aunt Debbie

"We want some pictures," Val explained.

I wasn't quite sure pictures of what.

"Of the birth," Val said.

I hid my, well, disapproval of such an idea. Take pictures of my sister Valerie's vagina and whatever came out of it? I remembered my shame at being completely naked—in deeper ways than just physically—and defenseless during Donald's birth.

Me and my sister Valerie are close in that we actually like each other and can talk easily. Love is a given. We each recognized the other as stubborn and bullheaded, but I wouldn't tell her that and she wouldn't tell me. Not in those words. I couldn't refuse Val's request, and agreed to take pictures of Valerie and Richard's baby being born, not for a moment imagining the dramatic proportions the event would assume.

I had finally gotten Donald in to see a pediatric neurologist in Decatur who concluded that Donald did not have not Down Syndrome. That was a good thing. But he couldn't tell what was causing the slow development. Donald, at a year, was just now cross-crawling.

"He cries every single morning when he wakes up, even though I am right there beside him," I tell the doctor. His name tag said Dr. Niter Makan. He had a British accent. "Do you have any further questions at this time, Madam?" he asked. I just stared at him. "What's wrong with my son?" I asked desperately.

"We will just have to watch and see how he does. Yes?"

Then he was out the door, which clicked shut.

Early Saturday morning on the ninth of July, during a weekend after Donald and I moved in with Val and Richard, I woke up to hear Val retching in their bedroom. "Don't worry about cleaning it up, Richard," Val said frantically. "Just get the goddamn hospital bag and let's go!" I was dressed in a minute, and Chandra Gupti, from next door, had already heard the commotion and was opening our front door with a key she kept for taking care of houseplants and a cat when we were away. Her responsibility today was Donald, who was dead to the world in the den where he and his mom stayed. Donald liked the way Chandra smelled and was always good when she was around.

On the drive to Douglasville, Val was experiencing painful contractions and the only way she could stand it was to kneel in the front passenger seat facing backwards, with her forehead resting on the seat back and her arms wrapped around the seat. Val barely had time between contractions to prepare for the next assault.

Shush

It was my Aunt Debbie, present at my birth to take photographs, who first laid hands on me. Or rather caught me when I shot through the birth canal head first and full speed ahead. The MD was still putting on his latex gloves, and the attendant midwife was so surprised at my exit velocity that she had little time to react. My dad stood in the next down-bed position. I caromed off his forearms. I must have felt, to those present, like a wet mackerel tossed in the air to see who could catch it.

Having made it past the network of grasping hands and the blur of astounded faces, I had no idea that my delivery into the world was fast becoming life threatening. Had it not been for Aunt Debbie's lightning-fast reactions, and had I not been tethered by my umbilical cord, I might have slid out the door and down the hallway.

Aunt Debbie's Pentax camera, the only thing of any real value she owned, slid from her hands as I was born. My birth was passing so quickly that my aunt, whom I would come to know as Donald's mother, hadn't secured the strap over her head and around her neck. If my eyes had been open and I could have seen the direction in which I was headed, I might have watched the camera falling in slow liquid motion from Aunt Debbie's sweaty hands to the hard tile floor of the birthing room, sounds of glass lenses breaking, metal pieces clanking on tile.

While the camera was falling, Aunt Debbie instinctively assumed the position of a middle linebacker just before the snap, crouched over slightly, and thus was able to catch me with her whole body, stopping my headlong journey against her soft, padded midsection. Aunt Debbie held me briefly, letting the midwife suction my nose and mouth. Somebody held me aloft like a dead rabbit, whereupon I performed my first aria and was placed on Mom's belly near enough to her breast that I could almost taste the liquid dripping warm from her nipples. At the same time I emptied my bladder.

As far as I was concerned, and based on my knowledge about this strange world so far, everything seemed to be going fairly well.

When, in fact, life just seemed to be getting more complicated. It didn't work out very well with Aunt Debbie and Donald staying with us. After I was born, I guess, Aunt Debbie started complaining that I was everyone's favorite, like it was some kind of popularity contest.

Dad helped Aunt Debbie find a pretty good job as a medical records stenographer through someone he knew in the pharmaceutical industry who had connections. My aunt, who I knew was a shot-putter, or had been in high school, was now setting all sorts of records in typing speed and accuracy. Aunt Debbie, also with Dad's help, found an inexpensive basement apartment in a bachelor Baptist preacher's house, and they moved there and from then on visited us on weekends.

Valerie

Richard wouldn't talk to me about it, of course, until the dirt could no longer be swept under the rug. At first I felt cold but understood that from his point of view, he had a sick wife, he needed some physical affection and intimacy, and neither of us had read very far into the books and brochures that tell chronically ill people and their spouses how to take care of themselves as well as each other.

Richard, c'mon. It was so obvious to everyone at work that I actually heard the gossip from another of your female co-workers who couldn't mind her own business.

Richard, I don't hate you for doing this. I'm too tired to respond like that. I can't really feel anything about you now. You are doing the heavy lifting on this one, pal. "For better or for worse. In sickness and in health." Ring a bell? Oh, I'm getting snippy because I feel so crappy. Some days, I swear, I'm this close. To what?

For the moment, let's say you get the hell out of the house. Go get an apartment somewhere. Don't call me. I'll call you. You figure it out, just like I had to figure out what to do a long time ago in a situation that was so unfair, it still pisses me off—and it's bigger than you'll ever know.

Leave me alone.

Shush

It might have had something to do with the Baptist preacher that sent our family into the fire and brimstone, but shortly after we'd relocated Aunt Debbie and Donald, all hell broke loose. My dad was being weird. He always came home from work telling us all how much he liked his job and wasn't life great?

He mentioned a particular woman at work he liked. I guessed, from what I overheard, they were having an affair. I found out from a girl at school who knew the woman's family. Dad was ashamed, I think, and was ready to pack a suitcase one day, presumably to abandon me and Mom in his remorsefulness. Dad knew that Mom was having a flare-up of her em-ess, but some part of his own brain must have been malfunctioning.

I heard Mom and Dad talking in loud whispers in their bedroom, the door partly open.

I went back to my bedroom, then made some noise to indicate that I was just emerging from it. Then Dad was leaving their room. "Dad, don't you love me and Mom anymore?"

"But I do love you, Eggy," he said with a stricken face. "Daddy made a big mistake."

"Dad, you're talking to me like I'm three." And I turned around and went into the kitchen to see if there was any peanut butter. I heard the door close behind my dad and started crying, believing myself responsible for the whole mess because I was so, so fast. The speed of time had something to do with it, somehow. I looked up at the kitchen clock. The second hand wasn't moving.

That night, Mom and Aunt Debbie held each other in our living room and cried and cried. They cried so much that I started crying too. I missed Dad, who moved to an apartment closer to his job. I visited him there and didn't like it. There was no stuff on the walls to make it look homey.

All of a sudden it seemed like everyone in my school was talking about something great they had done with their dad. Alice Peters, a fourth grader, said in the cafeteria one day during lunch that last weekend her dad took just her and not her brothers to Six Flags Over Georgia and they had a super time. She looked right at me. "So, Shush, what have you done with your dad that's fun?" Alice said, with sarcastic emphasis on the words *you* and *your*.

"Nothing. My dad committed suicide."

I don't know why I said it. I really don't, but it sure put me on the map when word got to my teacher and parents, and I had to go talk to a counselor.

I had to tell all my friends that that Dad only got a divorce, which made people feel better, but even that wasn't true. Dad was simply in exile.

Right after this, Mom had an exacerbation of her em-ess and felt angry at Dad for that too.

I think Dad didn't really know what to do. With himself, with

Mom's em-ess, with me. He might have been thinking about when Mom gets worse. I worried about that too.

I wonder why hard things take so long to work out. I have ambitions to make my own changes. I feel like I am ready to soar through the sky, free, weightless, going somewhere important and having a really great time getting to wherever that is.

I decided that Dad would just have to do what Mom said: figure it out.

Shush (continued)

To me, there was always something smelly and dark about Donald that I couldn't process, but I knew that he was a different animal altogether. Even when I was only five months old. I was not like him, I knew that much, and this realization marked my first major step in differentiating myself from others, especially boys. I began discerning sounds from Mom and Dad, sounds like *hurh* and *scheee* and *gurrel* that seemed to refer to me in some way, while other utterances sounded like they were directed at Donald or Dad. These latter sounds I chose to ignore, for the most part, until I was in high school.

Donald was a year older than me, and much larger physically. He could beat me up if he wanted to and if he could catch me. At five months I could cross-crawl faster than he could toddle on his two fat legs. Also, to my supreme advantage, I had an early intuitive understanding of manipulative behavior, while Donald was still clueless about using vocal pitch, eye movement, and facial expressions to convey irony, disbelief, pseudo-atonement—or any other attitudes that I found useful in dealing with my parents, in particular. Donald's repertoire of credible verbal and emotional expression ran from "I dinn do it!" to "Shush did it!"

I think it was Aunt Debbie's philosophy that if she just loved him enough, Donald would get better, that kids who are cherished turn out okay. Donald wasn't turning out too okay. Whenever they came over, usually on weekends, I tried to hide from Donald, ignore him, or pretend I had homework. Once, in a mean mood, after I said, "You aren't the sharpest pencil in the box," Donald threatened to stuff me into the trash can, which he was capable of doing. I no longer felt that my intellect provided me with any protection from Donald's size and strength.

Every day, just about, I pleaded with Mom to give Dad another chance. "I miss him," I said, "and Donald scares me. I'd feel safer having a man around the house." Mom said that Donald was taking Effexor to treat his *rage* issues, and that Aunt Debbie or her would always be nearby. They would never even leave me alone in a room with Donald, she said. The reassurance scared me even more.

"Do you still love Dad?" I asked.

Mom struggled with my question, I could see it. Finally, she turned around from the sink full of dirty dishes to face me, hanging on to the back of a chair for balance.

"Shush, I just really don't know. It hurts, what your dad did, okay? I'm just so glad to have you. Can't we be enough for now?"

No, I wanted to say, but instead I quietly decided that if I could do some great deed, or make a huge sacrifice, it would somehow reunite our family. It made sense if I didn't think about it too much. Like I didn't think very much about Donald when he wasn't around. I was only frightened when he was in our house, where he seemed to take on larger, more dangerous proportions. He was already as tall as Aunt Debbie, and sometimes I thought she was afraid of him too.

I got so mixed up with my crazy ideas about uniting the family that nothing made much sense.

The house felt really empty and quiet without Dad, even though if he were living here he'd still be at work. It was a deeper emptiness I felt, as though something essential had been pulled out of my body, and the place where it came from was just a gaping hole. And it wasn't just Dad. It was Mom's illness, which enraged her so much that it seemed she was actually hurting her chances of getting well. She had been to three neurologists, all of them offering her powerful disease-inhibiting treatments. Mom is as stubborn as her em-ess, but she finally agreed to take a limited amount of the proffered medication.

On Friday afternoon Aunt Debbie arrived with Donald before Mom got home from work. Donald looked to me like he was glazed and duller than usual.

When Mom got home from work, she was glad to see Aunt Debbie, who usually arrived on Saturday morning. They started to chat so I went over and sat next to Donald on the couch. When I waved my hand in front of his eyes, it was like nobody was home.

"Shush, honey," said Aunt Debbie, "you'd best just leave Donald alone. He had a little accident today and he's on some special medication right now." I don't know how I missed it, but I looked and saw that Donald's right hand was wrapped in and taped to some gauzy padding.

"What happened, Aunt Debbie, did he cut himself on something?"

"Shush," my mom said in a warning voice

"No, Valerie, I want to tell you. Donald hit another boy today with his fist. No reason. I had to leave work early to pick him up. Then he kicked a hole in his bedroom door. This is the worst it's been. I managed to calm him down enough to get him to take the Valium. Then I drove here. I don't know what to do."

I was scared that night that Donald would wake up and try to kill us all. After I'd gone to bed, I heard Mom and Aunt Debbie talking quietly in the kitchen. Then the screen-door on the front porch opened and shut and I heard Dad's voice! In a way, I wanted to rush into the kitchen and just hug him, but I also didn't want to interrupt the sense of security I felt with him just being home. I drifted easily into sleep.

In the morning, I was still alive. I got out of bed, anxious to know about Dad, but the only other person in the house was Mom. It was Saturday morning, so she still had on her bathrobe. I didn't ask where Donald was; I didn't even want to think about him. I think Mom felt the same way.

"Mom, are you going to let Dad coming back? I heard him in the kitchen last night."

"Your dad came to help your Aunt Debbie find a safe place for her and Donald to spend the night, is all."

Aunt Debbie

I also took to calling her Shush, as Valerie and Richard unofficially christened my niece. Her legal name is Elizabeth Susan McCrea; the Susan was for our younger sister who died when she was fourteen.

Shush was the gifted child, from the start. Donald was the dunce, or so I felt about how other people saw him.

He was getting worse. Donald and I were living in the preacher's basement apartment. I was just fixing dinner when Donald came out of his bedroom, furious that the show he wanted to watch on television wasn't on till tomorrow. "So you have something to look forward to," I suggested, turning to face him. He made a sound something like *nugghh* and pushed me in the chest with enough force that I fell down hard on my tailbone. There I sat, helpless to save my own child. I feared not for my safety but for his. Envisioning the pale green walls of the psychiatric ward Donald would never leave, I sat there on the floor while my son walked into the living room and tried to start a fire with a small pile of junk mail on the table, but couldn't make the matches light.

Shush

It took a month in the psychiatric program of a good facility in Decatur, which Aunt Debbie really couldn't afford, for Donald to respond to a new arsenal of medications and behavioral modifications, meeting every day with a counselor who worked with kids like Donald, kids who weren't bad, just sick in a way that made them hard and sometimes dangerous to be around. Kids with autism, or behavioral problems, or some kind of learning disorder.

It made me look at Donald in a different way, more as a broken thing that could be fixed with the right tools, than a damaged contribution to the scrap heap. Really, when I thought about it Donald was, like, just a family member who only wanted to be happy, or have the opportunity to be happy, like the rest of us.

That night, Mom asked Dad if he would mind coming over for dinner. Whatever kind of stuff they'd been doing to make up was working. Just hearing them talk like they used to talk together, being real, gave me some hope that a kind of peace might be at hand. I didn't let my hopes get too high.

For my eleventh birthday, I told Mom and Dad that I wanted to go to the circus.

"The circus," said Dad, as if he had never heard the word before. "Don't they abuse animals at circuses?"

I thought of Mom's story, about the circus guy she'd met before I was born, and wondered if she'd ever told Dad. It felt strange knowing something about Mom that Dad didn't know. It made Dad seem smaller somehow, not as all-knowing as I'd believed.

My request struck a chord in Mom. "I assume," she said, trying to sound light and playful, "that you fully researched this idea and have a full itinerary ready for our review."

Mom's em-ess was taking a toll on her vision, and she sometimes used a nonpowered wheel chair when her legs weren't working. She was too tired to put much energy into hating it. The vision problem gave her face an odd kind of blankness. She was currently taking amantadine, Avonex, Elavil, Wellbutrin, and a short course of prednisone whenever things got really bad.

"Actually," I said, "the only time that's anywhere even close to my birthday, they'll be in Terre Haute. It's the Red Tour, which is supposed to be the best one."

"Terre Haute," said Dad, trying to be funny, doing a lousy southern accent. "That's Yankee territory. Lutherans live there, I've heard."

"What are you saying, Richard," my mom interrupted, edgy in her wheelchair.

"It was a joke, Val—you left Minnesota when you were eighteen because you couldn't stand it. Terre Haute is north of Atlanta. That's all. I'm sorry, it's stupid."

"People can change. I'm a different person than I was then. It might help to be in a cooler climate now."

"Okay, I've apologized. But Shush, that's a pretty big trip."

I stayed out of it now that the trip had become part of an adult dialogue where they said things that seemed to mean something else.

"I would personally love to see the circus," Mom said with a sudden smile. "I think we should do it. But I have a suggestion. I've done a little checking on my own, and the same show is in Little Rock a week earlier. It's the Blue Tour."

I stared dumbfounded at Mom. Finally I said, "It is? We can see it in Little Rock. That's fine with me."

"Little Rock, Arkansas?" Dad said.

"Du-uh," I responded.

"The only other question …" began Mom.

I was ready for this. "I think Aunt Debbie and Donald should come too," I said.

That seemed to make Mom happy. Dad was resigned to the idea and didn't dare say anything more. After all, he was still on probation. He had promised Mom that the affair was over, and she took him on his word, I guess. Dad realized that for him and Mom this was a very important trip.

During the three weeks leading up to our journey to Little Rock, I went to the library and looked in the *Guinness Book of World Records* to see what the distance record for flight was by a human cannonballer. I was just curious. It took me a while, but I found it: on May 29, 1998, David "Cannonball" Smith flew 185 feet and 10 inches somewhere in Pennsylvania.

I learned that the cannon didn't really "shoot" anyone anywhere, it launched them using hydraulic springs and made some smoke for show, but the speed was real; they flew at seventy miles an hour. Sometimes they blacked out and didn't come to early enough to turn belly side up for the landing in the net. The chances of a human cannonball dying on the job were 50 per cent.

I knew it was farther than 185 feet and 10 inches from Atlanta to Douglasville, the first trip I'd taken in my life, which I think I owe, besides to Mom and Dad, to Aunt Debbie. She was my safety net.

Mom really made a fuss about going *past* Little Rock to Hot Springs, to spend a day and a night. "It's such a nice town," Mom said to Dad. I was there once a lifetime ago, but I loved it." Dad looked at me. We just barely rolled our eyes so Mom wouldn't notice. I figured Mom was thinking about the guy she met there before I was born. I wasn't really sure, but I was sort of keeping an eye on Mom in case she started to lose it. I'd seen her get more fragile this year.

The road trip in our Dodge Caravan, filled with five people and our baggage, from Atlanta to Hot Springs took longer than Dad had anticipated. It was a pitch black night, and we were on a smaller state highway, far from the interstate, winding through a landscape I could only imagine from the turns, dips, and rises of the road. Lightning flashed, followed by a crack of thunder, and the skies opened. It was raining as hard as I'd ever seen rain fall, and yet a ground fog had set in at the same time.

"Damn!" Dad said. "I have never seen anything like this." His face was grim with concentration on the partially visible road ahead. It had been a while since we had passed any building—a house, a store, a gas station. Mom, who was sitting in the seat next to Dad's, until now had been stone still. She turned to her left.

"Richard, do you think we should just stop the car and wait it out?" But Dad pressed ahead. "We'll get to something soon," he said, and he was actually reassuring, the old Dad I could look up to and trust.

Mom put her hand on the back of his neck and gave him a little massage, and I could see in the rear view mirror that he smiled at the attention.

After taking a wide arcing curve at 25 mph, the road straightened and we saw the lights of a small town, more like a settlement or outpost. Few lights shone in the windows, but I could see Confederate flags as our headlights grazed the old wooden structures. Here, in the middle of nowhere, was a motel with a single vacancy. We took it, and got Mom wheeled inside. The walls were knotty pine, and there was even a small television. The motel clerk, probably the owner's kid, wheeled in an extra folding bed for Donald, and Aunt Debbie insisted on sleeping on her camping pad on the floor. Dad gave the clerk a five. That made the kid smile.

We all showered, Mom with help from Dad, who was being so careful with her fragile and noncompliant body. Then we watched part of a college football game on the television. There was barely enough room for the five of us, but we seemed not to mind. Dad discovered a cafe that was open next to the motel. In a while, we would go get something to eat.

"Shush," said Dad, "can you take these wet towels back to the office and see if we can get some dry ones?"

Picking up the still warm, damp towels, I scooted out and under the awning across the face of the motel. It was still raining pretty hard. Tomorrow, I thought, the sun would rise and shine brightly on the surrounding forest, on the motel sill glistening with moisture, and on our family, as we continued our journey to the circus. The circus! It seemed like things were going to work out after all. This was going to be a good trip.

Just before I dashed into the office, I noticed for the first time the name of the motel displayed in bright red neon. How had I missed it when we drove up? It must have been the excitement and relief of finding a safe haven during such a terrible storm.

While the woman behind the counter brought out clean, dry towels, I wondered where we were.

"Tell your Dad that I'll have to charge extra for the clean laundry," she told me.

"Are we anywhere near the Mason-Dixon line?" I asked.

She nodded up at the neon motel sign and laughed.

"Don't let the name of this *moe*-tel fool you, darlin'," she answered. "You ain't even close."

Forgotten Wife

The old wife, older than anyone could know or even imagine, had cooked so many pots of soup, greens, beans, prairie grains and prairie dogs, onions, raccoon tail, and caribou tongue in the black cast-iron pot, cleaning and scrubbing after each use with a stiff bristle brush made of a hundred porcupine quills, that one day she scrubbed right through the bottom of the pot. Never had she heard about anybody scrubbing clean through cast iron cooking pots, and if it had happened, she would have known about it. Obviously, something funny was going on here, and as the wash water drained out of the pot through the hole she'd made with the porcupine quill brush, she knew something magical was going to happen.

This was in the days of trade in beaver pelts and other animal skins, and in the days of the Trails of Tears and "I will fight no more forever" and "as long as the rivers shall run," the time of broken promises and nightmares when the People were dying of smallpox. The survivors were put on forced march to live in the worst corners of creation, given seeds and hand-implements for farming, and cast-iron cooking pots and blankets that carried the smallpox—blankets disguised as protection against the cold. The white dogs also killed the People with their guns. That is how the old wife lost her son in the battle at Little Creek.

As the old wife examined the pot carefully to check for signs of such magic, she held it up to her face and looked through the hole, which was about the size of the full moon when it is directly overhead. She peered and peered, and after a minute her dead son walked through the door. At least he had been dead, ever since Little Creek, in a battle that the People fought by the river she had lived near since as far back as she could remember. And that was a long time ago. But here he was, well and alive, as she could plainly see.

"Mother, why are you looking at me through a hole in that old pot?" the son asked.

"What kind of magic brought you here, son?" his mother asked in astonishment.

The old wife finally put the pot down on the plain wooden

table, and placed the brush made with one hundred porcupine quills on the small ledge near the fire.

"What kind of question would that be?" the son demanded.

The old wife shrugged submissively.

"Mother, I can't stay long, if you know what I mean," the son said in a more gentle voice. "But I have a favor to ask."

"What kind of favor?" she asked, suspicious even though this person did look like her son. She caught a whiff of horse testicles frying, but she had not been cooking horse testicles and wondered if it was a sign of trouble.

"Would you take care of my own son, just a small child who has never really belonged with the People?"

Suddenly, beside the old wife's son, there appeared a boy not much more than five or six summers. He was shy and looked at the floor, not meeting his grandmother's eyes.

And before the old wife could say anything to indicate whether she would agree to this strange adoption, her son walked out the door and was never seen again walking the earth. The old wife looked at the boy, sighed, and realized that she might as well add another 25 years to the life she'd nearly finished, to properly raise this little imp, who suddenly looked up, gazing into her dark eyes with his own, and said, "I've always lived with dead people before. They don't eat much. I'm very hungry."

The old wife's husband had died from the smallpox many summers back. It was too long ago for most people to remember. His other, younger wives had died too, the ones who tanned the caribou hides with urine and deer brains, made moccasins out of the softened and scraped leather, and bore his children, all dead now from one thing or another. But by the time the younger wives died, they had aged dramatically and had become hags and crones, while the old wife looked to be an indeterminate age, not young, but not the grayhair she should have been after so many winters.

Even though she lived alone, a two-days' walk to anywhere, the old wife was still regarded by the People with a certain distant respect. It was rare to see her about more than once every couple years. She was given wide berth, because some feared that she traded in spells and curses, which was nonsense.

And now she had a grandson. This was a hope she had given up years ago. Her dead son was the only child of her husband's, borne by her, who had lived longer than a few months beyond birth.

Why was she being given this boy, she wondered. Something troubled her about the whole situation, but she was kept so busy—feeding the boy from her shrinking supply of forage, making him clothing from scraps of wool and other cloths, as well as animal hides and tightly woven prairie grasses, whatever she had or could find, and teaching him to forage for roots and fashion arrows so he could hunt with the bow that the old wife's husband had once used to kill game—that she had little time to waste on vague fears.

There was plenty to do. She forgot about her misgivings, and for the first time as far back as she could remember, she felt happiness.

She called the boy Grandson. She could not think of another name that fit, partly because of the odd circumstances surrounding his appearance. If her son had been a ghost, then her grandson could be either dead or alive, on the side of light or the side of darkness. But the old wife did not fear darkness. She had suffered in darkness before.

Having lived among dead people for such a long time, Grandson exhibited some strange, troubling qualities. For example, at night he slept on his back only, like a corpse, and didn't move all night. The old wife sat by his side one night to see if he would turn to the side or snore, or perhaps talk in his sleep. Not only did he not move a muscle or utter a sound; he seemed to be just barely breathing. For moments at a time his breathing stopped, and she jumped back when she touched his cold hand.

When he slept in this world, the old wife reasoned, he lived in the other world, the land of the dead.

In the morning, Grandson got up, went outside to relieve himself, and came back inside. It was always the same request, issued casually, with the enthusiasm of an active boy: "I'm hungry. Can we eat?" Then the day began to roll along on its familiar course, and the old wife forgot about how frightened she had been when she felt his hand the night before. It was as if his veins were filled with ice water.

Spring and summer had passed since Grandson first showed up at the old wife's cabin, and the cold times would come soon. The old wife had to walk for two days to the trading post to exchange skins of animals caught in her traplines for another black cast iron pot. She asked Grandson to kill some game and they would feast when she returned from her journey in four or five days.

At the white dog's outpost, which she reached in the afternoon of her second day of trekking, she saw no other People. The white agent at the remote station, the only other soul around, asked what had happened to the cooking pot he'd traded to her four years ago.

"I remember you," he said.

The old wife just shrugged, not used to being known or asked questions, especially by this smelly white ghost. Laying the skins, poor ones, on the counter in trade, she put the cooking pot, a new sewing needle, and a spool of cotton thread into her pack and backed away from the agent.

"No candy, old wife?" the agent said as she continued backing out the door.

The old wife stiffened.

"A nice rifle for you, some tobacco or maybe some of the dried corn I have packed into bags?"

She felt the chill of supernatural presence. Bad magic breathed outward with the agent's voice. "I remember you. Your son got killed at Little Creek."

"How can you know that?" the old wife asked, straightening her body so her face looked like it was floating above her neck.

"Because I saw him get shot," said the agent.

The old wife's breath left her as though she had been hit in the stomach by a thundering bull calf. But she tried not to show her pain. She simply shrugged again and turned to leave. At her back, she heard the agent's voice, "Be careful, old wife, there's no one out there to take care of you."

That was one thing the old wife and the white dog agent agreed on.

She stopped that night, halfway home, and ate a piece of dried hare meat, which gave her some strength to gather grasses into a kind of bed. Fearing that the white dog agent might be following her, she made no fire, drank only a little of the water she'd carried from the spring at home, and was on her way again before the stars faded.

Walking toward home, she thought about the quality and strength of the magic, but when Grandson appeared at the door and smiled, she forgot her worries and showed him the new pot.

"Can we eat? he said immediately. "I'm hungry."

"Yes, my Grandson," she answered, proud and happy to at last be a grandmother. "Now I can cook stew with onions I have gathered and with the game you have killed."

Grandson looked down at the floor and confessed that he had already consumed the quail, snake, fox, ermine, and prairie dog that he had killed with his father's bow, shooting the arrows he himself had fashioned from the wood of the white oak that grew at the edges of the old wife's known world.

"I couldn't wait," he said with a guilty grin, from which fresh blood trickled. "And still I am hungry. Can we eat?"

The old wife remembered the time when in a dream she saw white dogs without eyes chasing an elk across the low, gently rising and falling terrain. The dogs were howling. "We can't see! We can't see!" they cried, trying to trick the elk into stopping. But the elk knew better about the dogs with no eyes and kept running. Eventually, they passed over a rise and were gone. The old wife was scared at first, but when the dogs disappeared over the last hill, her fear vanished and she slept soundly.

The old wife couldn't remember what had happened the day after the dream, or what it might mean, or why it had come to mind at this particular time. Now, she saw nothing but Grandson standing before her. The blood had disappeared from the smooth skin of his face. He looked like a growing boy, and she was pleased that he had warmed to his grandmother over the past year.

"Grandmother, is something the matter?" Grandson asked the old wife. "You look strange."

And at those words, spoken in a soft voice, the old wife forgot about what troubled her. Before cooking some prairie onions and reddish sweet-tasting tubers, she scrubbed out the new cast-iron cooking pot to get the white dog smell off of it, using water from the spring and the scrubber made with one hundred porcupine quills.

"I need to be very careful," she said to herself. "This situation requires delicacy."

For the next week, she was careful to keep Grandson well fed, cooking him hearty stews with elk loin chunks, onions, and herbs she knew would calm her grandson and keep him peaceful and mildly tranquilized. The thing the herbs did not do was slake his appetite.

She had not been able to find evidence of his digestive process, even after a methodical search for his scat that she had performed one afternoon, looking in widening circles around the cabin.

The following day, the old wife was sitting outside in the sunlight trying to loop thread through the eye of her new steel needle.

"My eyes are worse this year," she said aloud, because she was tired of silence.

As the old wife tried again with the thread, she saw a strange creature approaching. As the indistinct figure moved closer to where she was sitting, the old wife realized it was a boy, four or five summers old. Even before he came within an afternoon shadow's distance of her straight-backed chair, which had been tossed from a wagon train passing this way years ago, she smelled the white dog in him. It was mixed with the sweetgrass aroma of the living People. This combination she had noticed only once before, when she stood beside the bastard white dog scout who had helped plan the Little Creek attack. The scout could have killed her, but had enough of the People in his blood to harbor fearful second thoughts about the implications that might ensue, if not in this world, then in the spirit realm.

The old wife decided that if she ever encountered the scout again, which she realized was highly unlikely, she would kill him.

The boy stopped a few paces away. The old wife still held the needle and thread in front of her, like a spirit shield.

She noted that the boy's ribs stuck out, his belly was distended, and his legs and arms were twigs. But in his eyes there was a flicker of brownish orange light, like a wolf's eyes, showing him to be alert.

"Are you also my son's child?" the old wife asked in a voice that expressed her dread that this could be the case.

He just stared into her eyes and said nothing.

"Are you alive or dead?" she asked.

The boy spoke some words in a strange tongue the old wife had never heard. The inflection at the end of his utterance suggested a question. Moving slowly towards the old wife, he reached out carefully and coaxed her to release the needle and thread, whereupon he pushed the thread through the needle's eye on his first attempt. They both smiled.

"I am making my spirit bundle," she told the boy, who only looked blankly at her.

In spite of the dubious status of this new arrival, and despite her concern with magical events that seemed to be occupying more and more of her attention, the old wife was pleased to start sewing a scrap of wool blanket and some old trade ribbon to make the small bag that would carry her power objects: the stone from Little Creek that carried the People's memory of that place. The lock of her husband's hair she'd cut with his steel-bladed knife, touching him even though he was blistering with the pox. Two rattlesnake fangs she had extracted from a piece of firewood that the serpent had hit, a miscalculation that proved to be fatal to the viper. Its target was the hand that held the stick, but with its fangs thus implanted, the old wife had been able to crush the snake's head with a rock.

She also carried dried and ground nightshade leaves, to be used in the event that her spirit power were to fail before she was done with her body. The body itself was of little importance.

The old wife called the new boy White Dog.

The strange family foraged and hunted through the late, unusually warm fall, drying the meat of antelope, porcupine, pheasant, and small wetland fowl in small strips that cured faster than thick slabs. Tubers and onions and edible roots were gathered by the old wife, who knew where to look for them.

While out on the sparsely forested land to the north one day, deciding whether the white root she was looking at was poisonous or nutritious, she began to wonder if Grandson would ever say anything besides "I'm hungry. Can we eat now?" She cursed her dead son for leaving her with this burden, but smiled when in her mind she saw Grandson's face, which was beginning to fill out. Grandson would look like his father.

For his part, White Dog readily took his place at the bottom of the family hierarchy and did his share of the work. He spoke occasionally in his strange language that the old wife feared might be a tongue through which spells could be cast. She did not appreciate hearing his gibberish, and when she really wanted him to stop, she looked at him, frowned, and drew her finger across the front of her neck with a slicing motion. They both understood this language clearly.

As the first snow of that winter at last began to blow across the prairie from the north, with little to get in its way for hundreds of miles except a few scraggly trees, the old wife, Grandson, and White

Dog all worried that there was not enough of anything: food, blankets, warm clothes, or wood and dung for the fire.

"There is not enough to carry us through, even with game to kill," Grandson said. "We can't live on rabbits. We will eat through our carefully prepared rations within weeks."

White Dog snorted. He, more then either of the other two, knew true hunger, when the body begins to consume its own flesh and bones.

The boy was saying something incomprehensible on this topic, the old wife guessed, when there was a knock at the cabin door.

"Grandson, ask who is there and unlatch the door, the old wife said.

Again there was another knock, patient as the wind.

"Make White Dog unlatch the door," Grandson said peevishly, pointing first at the younger boy, then at the door. White Dog rose slowly, terrified at what he might see when he pushed open the door. He knew of White Buffalo Calf Woman, who appeared to mortals as a beautiful maiden, and whose powers of compassion as well as retribution were great. He had been with the followers of White Buffalo Calf Woman for many seasons, always at the edge of the firelight. Knowing his blood to be impure only added to his fear of whoever, or whatever, was on the other side of the door.

The young woman standing outside the cabin, Janie Luck, did not start out as a ghost. That came later, after the People had lost their traditions and dignity.

Of her birth, she remembered red, pools of red, eyes full of redness. Being hungry, and the cold, bloodless breast of her mother. Rigid flesh, stiffening as the newborn lay against the dead body. The grandmother finally intervened, lifting the child and giving the tiny body what little warmth she could still provide.

Had it been left to the People, the baby would have been allowed to die in the cold, her remains left to be scavenged by wolves and ravens. Another mouth to feed.

Instead, she survived and was raised by her grandmother.

Fourteen summers later, Janie Luck, beautiful and much desired by the young men among the People, was raped by a white dog soldier during the massacre at Little Creek. The soldiers forced the surviving People to relocate to a land that was inhospitable and soaked in the blood of battles, and they were advised to grow crops or starve. It was at this place that Janie Luck gave birth to a half-breed male child, the one the old wife would call White Dog a few years later.

When he was a year old, due to pressure from the People, who could never accept the mongrel white dog as one of their own, Janie Luck, doing the only thing that came to mind, brought the child to the people of the White Buffalo Calf Woman, who lived in a remote river valley that had not yet been taken by the white dogs. These People still had magical powers, which they kept well hidden, and used only when necessary to defend their faith and land. They were excellent at hiding and well drilled in the art of ambush.

As the young woman began to knock a third time, she heard the latch lift. The door began to open.

She stood in the doorway, staring at White Dog, whose skin turned an even paler shade.

The woman's face, visible to the old wife in the glow of the fire, had prominent high cheekbones. Her hair was midnight black, and the light from the burning embers showed her color to be a golden brown, with reddened cedar-bark cheeks and nose marking how cold she was.

Regarding the young woman skeptically, the old wife decided that she was no danger and that the stranger might well be one of the People.

"Honored grandmother," said the young woman, "may I come in and sit at your fire?"

At least she has good manners, thought the old wife.

"Yes, grand-daughter, come inside and rest," the old wife answered, using the formal and correct manner of speech that two women of different generations are taught from a young age to employ in greeting and welcoming. In fact, it was considered very rude either to ask for a name or to identify oneself by name before an appropriate amount of time had passed.

At least these were the customs before the People had lost hope, tradition, and dignity.

The young woman spoke the language of the People perfectly,

a fact that somewhat reassured the old wife. But by this point she had to wonder why, after a lifetime of almost complete solitude, she was suddenly attracting young people to her home the way a dead horse left to rot out on the prairie draws ravens and vultures.

The young woman, the old wife estimated, had seen eighteen or nineteen springs. She seemed mature and self-assured as she came inside, squatted down, and put her open hands close to the stove. The old wife invited her to share their meal of squirrel breast, preserved duck eggs, skqa-nik roots and prairie onions. The meal was simmering in the cast-iron cooking pot.

A look of distaste passed over the young woman's face. Only the old wife noticed. Perhaps she is used to different food, the old wife thought.

Although the boy White Dog was uneasy, he remained silent. He wasn't sure he wanted it confirmed that this person was known to him.

As for the old wife, she simply shrugged, no longer astonished at the strange course things were taking.

"The People know me by the name Janie Luck," the young woman began. As she spoke, Grandson began to hone in on Janie Luck's beauty, and felt a pleasant disturbance in his crotch.

"My old grandmother heard the name Janie from the mouth of a dying white dog soldier whom she had just skewered with a sharpened hardwood pole during a fierce battle shortly after I was born, one of many battles with the well-armed and ruthless white dog soldiers. She poked him between his ribs, then yanked the lance around in his guts until the white dog's eyes rolled back into his head and blood began to bubble from his mouth. The white dog managed to say one word before he fell over dead. *Janie*.

"At least that's the way Grandmother told the story to me."

Grandson and White Dog murmured, "I believe it. I believe it," which was proper etiquette after hearing a personal story, especially one involving death.

But the old wife seemed disgruntled.

"How did you come to be in this neck of the woods, wandering around in the dark on the night of the first snow?" she asked, thinking a coincidence to be unlikely.

"I follow the dead," Janie Luck explained.

"Well," said the old wife, "you're doing a very good job."

Grandson laughed nervously at this, while White Dog's face showed nothing.

"It's easy once you've learned to track," Janie Luck continued. "I've seen signs and smelled odors you never even knew you'd left. I've followed you all the way from Little Creek. To you, that seems long ago, but time is like the sun, endlessly repeating the same path."

When she was still very young and with the People, Janie Luck knew the old wife's name, Forgotten Wife, and was aware that her husband had died of smallpox. At one point during the journey of sorrow and defeat following Little Creek, Forgotten Wife simply disappeared. Where once she had journeyed with the People to more abundant parts of the prairie, she had seen only ghosts making this trip to a barren land, and she chose not to walk with them another step. She had no living relations. Forgotten Wife decided she would live just a little while longer. Forgotten is what she hoped to remain.

But that was not to be.

"I know you. You are Forgotten Wife," Janie Luck stated.

The old wife gasped for air. Was Janie Luck some kind of sorceress who had stolen memories of her son's death? Had she stopped and conversed with the white dog trader, who seemed to know so much about her—more than she'd ever told him?

Or was she a ghost?

"Your sorrow has been easy to follow," said Janie Luck. "But I've been in no hurry to find you, until recently."

The old wife suddenly felt a chill even in the warmth of the close cabin. It frightened her, this feeling of illness. As she slowly rocked herself forward and backward in her chair, something became clear.

"Here I am," she thought, "co-habiting with three ghosts, ghosts begotten by ghosts."

"I'm hungry," Grandson interrupted with his characteristic hopeful grin. "Can we eat now?" Grandson had forgotten the crisis of not enough food and supplies to last the winter; seemed to have forgotten that he was dead and had no worries or appetites, aside from those that he had borrowed from life.

The old wife was barely able to croak the words: "Yes, eat."

To no one in particular, perhaps more to Janie Luck than to the others, she whispered, "I think I need to lie down. I don't want any food tonight."

"Rest well, old wife," said Janie Luck.

Outside the snow began collecting in and around the old rusting cast-iron pot with the hole in the bottom. The old wife had simply tossed it out of the cabin when she returned from her journey to the trading post, where she laid out poorly cured skins to trade for the things she needed.

The spirit bag lay next to the blanket on which Forgotten Wife lay. It still needed a little work. With the cabin otherwise so still, the choking sobs of Forgotten Wife stood out. Carefully, White Dog, the starving boy with mixed blood, moved closer to the stove, closer to the mother he didn't completely trust, but was glad to see.

By morning, the old pot with the hole in the bottom would be covered by knee-high fresh snow, which had fallen throughout the night. The sun would rise on a world turned completely, magically white.

Waiting for Zero

In my grotesque vision of that which binds us, Mother is Captain Hook; Wendy is, well ... Wendy; Bob the transit driver is John Darling, Wendy's brother. Tinkerbelle? I don't know. And who am I? A make-believe pirate or a Class III sex offender? A recidivist, or a wide receiver?

In custody, I am allowed a visit with Wendy and a public defender. I am on their *caseloads*. Perhaps. Words and phrases fly towards me: *legal insanity, coercion, perjury, non-credible witnesses, circumstantial evidence, DNA forensics*, and so on.

I don't say anything. Nothing good, nothing good to say.

Wendy and the public defender try to help me. I appreciate that. But if I'm locked up again, I'll kill myself.

I apologize, Hank, says Wendy. I shouldn't have been so involved. It wasn't fair to you.

It sounds like a line from a movie.

But here's the good side. Captain Hook has been banished to cartoonland, at least while my medications hold.

Undetermined is the fate of Zero. I know what I did to the little prick, but no one can talk to me about it until the trial.

More on the bad side: Wendy is leaving my life, for professional reasons. I think I understand, but I like Wendy and feel sad about her departure from my life, such as it is. I'm really going to miss her.

I write this in my sketchbook on the bus one day.

... and my mother came unto me seated at the dining room table. Her hands were upon my shoulders, and although the pressure was light, I felt the talons and smelled blood, smelled the fried onions, the freshly baked bread, and the roasted chicken. My mother removed her hands from my shoulders, went to her chair and sat down.

Let us pray, she said.

All present bowed our heads.

Dear Lord, my mother began, we're just so grateful to You for all that You have provided for us. And Lord, we also feel especially blessed to have our Hank back home. You watched over him during that difficult time, and only You can tell if he learned his lesson. We know you would not make him suffer any more than needed. Your death and resurrection is and always will be our salvation. In the name of Jesus, Amen.

My mother is so full of Christian bullshit you could shovel it out the door and you'd still be standing ankle deep in it. At least that's my perspective. I sometimes wonder if my lack of faith, or sacrilegious sense of humor, inspired God to mold me as the dwarfish young adult whose small body and preternaturally boyish face could give a stranger the impression that I am a dangerous freak. God would have seen me coming, right? He would have had time to think about my soul and its corporeal manifestation. I've never thought of myself as deviant. I was created in God's image, just like everybody else.

I don't always like my life and my story. So I look at it in the only way I can look at it. It's what it is, and change is limited by fate, genetics, and whether one's mother is an evangelical, bible-thumping Christian fundamentalist—and, perhaps, a woman who drank heavily while I was in the womb. I'm just guessing. What my mother glossed over in her gripping homily is the fact that I was in prison for two years, serving time on a sexual-molestation-of-a-minor charge that the county prosecutor scratched out of the dirt to get me convicted on.

I was released the day before my twenty-fourth birthday.

Exactly what started happening to my brain while I was incarcerated had little to do with my sentence, my alleged crime, or my mother. Indeed, I noticed that I was forgetting things, getting disoriented in my cell, and feeling huge anxiety that went beyond the standard levels of mistrust and paranoia that eat away at you while living with people who don't like you and could hurt you badly at any time.

You want real-life experience? Prison is a bad choice. Just sit where you are, believe that you're safe, and, I'll tell you what, trouble will find you. That's as real as getting plugged with a shank on your way back to the cell you call home.

The neurologist they allow me to see orders an MRI and other tests, including a full blood panel. They finally settle on a diagnosis of young-onset Lewy-body dementia, with at least two major co-morbidity features: memory loss and, in my case, aural and visual hallucinations that may indicate a helping of paranoid schizophrenia.

It's getting worse. This is the first, and probably the last, story that you will hear from me, so you may wish to pay attention, which is more than I have done in my life.

Day Zero
First, I want you to know that I am not a misogynist. I respect women. And so, I genuinely enjoy it when Wendy Wentworth, MSW, comes over to visit me at The Home. At one of the recovering sex-offenders programs, Wendy leads the discussion on recidivism, a topic I am not that comfortable thinking about. After the meeting I ask if she is married, even though I see the ring. She laughs.

She comes to see just me, not any of the other half-wits and really messed-up men who take up space under this roof. I am a client in Wendy's caseload and she is nice. She's not trying to make me better. She just talks to me. She says that's her job. There are other inmates here, but they don't get to talk to Wendy.

Why do you do this? I ask.

What?

Try to help people like me.

Who are these people like you? Wendy asks.

The ones in prison, I say.

That's why I do this, she said. Now I get to ask you a question. What do you get out of fooling people about who you are?

That's easy, I say. I'm scared of who I am.

After Wendy leaves, days and days go by, and as the past unreels behind me, it is immediately gone, out of my reach. I know there is a past, and I've come to refer to this void as *Yesterday*. I may think I am moving forward from moment to moment into the future, but really it's just that Yesterday's getting bigger, and it pushes me so that it feels like I am only moving ahead. But I'm not. Does that make sense?

I have a theory. Nothing ever really happens to me, because, increasingly, I can't remember anything happening to me. There is a result without an apparent cause.

Clearly, I lack a moral context as well.

Day One

Thus I find myself standing on the sidewalk with my bus pass in my right hand on a Monday morning, holding my lunch bag and ready to experience my first day on my new job. I feel like a first grader, something that encourages me because it means I still have a conscious *perspective*. Rain falls and I have on my yellow jacket. I know what to do. The bus comes to a stop but I wait until it makes a *pppfff-ssshhh* sound and the front of the bus kneels down. I like that sound. Smiling, I get on the bus and slide my bus pass through the slot. I say to the bus driver, Hello, I'm Hank. He says he thought he recognized me and smiles. I'm only half-playing the fool, disguising myself in an idiot's face until I can figure out my next mask.

How did I arrive at this moment? Somehow, I got referred to The Home, a halfway house for vets and other men halfway to nowhere. We have some brain-damaged Iraq war vets, a couple guys who've done time, including me, and a second-offense con who is losing his memory.

On the good side, I have detected no riot-suppression equipment at The Home. It's not a prison, they say. Also on the good side: I get to visit with Wendy Wentworth once a week.

So I ride the bus. From Ride-the-Bus class I know just what to do when I ride. I can learn by repetition, which is not as unreliable as memory. The Director and Wardens make us do the same thing at the same time every day, pounding into us the routine of daily life. Like being in the Boot, but for the most part less dangerous.

I make friends with one of the bus drivers. His name is Bob. Bob gives me chewing gum one day. Wrigley's Spearmint. I take it, thinking I should bark like a dog so everybody on the bus knows something is definitely strange about me. We're not allowed to chew gum at The Home, but Bob says I can chew it on the bus, if I put it into the wastebasket up near his seat when I get out. The flavor's gone by then, anyway.

The bus is fun, I have to admit to myself, wondering which part of me is thinking this thought—the part that is disappearing but still aware, or the empty-headed dwarf trying to figure out how to open a door, maybe even wondering what a door is.

I see fat people, skinny people, crazy people, wizards and bums, people wearing sunglasses, angry people, nice people—all different, people who get off and on each time we stop. There's always something to look at on the bus. Nobody pretends to be interested in anything. But even the ads over the windows are enjoyable to me.

At the downtown depot, on my way to work, I meet Sissel, Glenden, and Zero. They're total low-lifes, so I decide to make friends with them, and they ask for money. I am going to work at Martins, an independent office-supply store downtown. It is the first job I've had out of prison, but I don't get to use the money I make. The director at The Home is in charge of all my money. I get an allowance, but I don't have any money to give these punks.

You see, they think I am, literally, demented.

I like to draw on the bus with a pencil in my notebook. To appear simple, I draw flowers, sunshine, and my mom. Then when I'm at home, I color the pictures in: red flowers, yellow sunshine, and black mom. I think black makes her look pretty again. I am beginning to hear her voice in my head. Just like I see shadow-shapes of animals at the edge of my vision—dogs and cats, harbingers of less subtle hallucinations, according to my prognosis.

At the bus station, Zero, Sissel, and Glenden are off to one side of the parked buses. They see me see them and Zero uses his index finger in a "come here" way, and I walk over to see them.

Hi Zero, I say.

Zero doesn't say anything. He never does, unless he's coming up with some big philosophical insight like, This is what I do, or Are we fucking clear what's going down?

Remember, Dumbo, we told you to bring money, Glenden says.

Zero takes the notebook away from me, looks through it and frowns. What the fuck is this?

I don't say anything.

You want this back? Zero says. I nod.

Well, to get it back you're going to have to do something for me, he says. Like an audition. And I'm going to watch you. Isn't that a fact? he says.

That's a fact, I repeat. That's another of Zero's annoying favorites. But I play the game.

Glenden laughs. He is the biggest one of the three and Zero is the smallest. Glenden says, He fuckin' says he'd do it. So what's the plan, Z?

Zero looks at me like he hates me.

Not my bitch, Glenden says. C'mon Z, it's your big fuckin' idea.

Zero pages through my sketch pad again, like he's looking for something.

What's this, he says, stopping at the page with the picture of my mom.

That's my mother, I answer.

Why is she all black? Zero says. Is your mom a nigger?

I don't say anything.

Are you a nigger? Zero says. I tell him I don't know.

Sissel tells Zero, You're in a fuckin' great mood today. Zero just glares at him. I tell them I have to go to work, but the balance of power is not on my side, and I couldn't escape without hurting someone. I've got to get into work by nine, operate the paper shredder by first using the *On* switch and then making sure it's set to *Forward*. I've been through a rigorous training session. I love the job because there is always a big pile of papers for me to shred, one by one, and it gives me time to think about what I'm going to do with the rest of my life.

It's okay, Dumbo, we'll give you a ride, Glenden says.

Then we are moving and I am moving with Glenden, Sissel, and Zero.

I really have to go to work, I warn them.

Glenden is the driver of the scratch 'n dent Outback. I sit in back between Zero and Sissel, and they are both silently looking out their windows in opposite directions.

Love is what makes a Subaru a Subaru, I say, twiddling my neurons.

Nobody speaks.

We are moving down the street now, away from the bus station, away from Bob, away from all the different people who ride the bus, away from my ironic sense of safety.

I am not supposed to ride the bus alone, according to the rules of The Home.

Nothing good, nothing good will come of this.

We are in the car for a while. I don't say anything.

Drive to my sister's apartment, Zero says. Glenden sees Zero in the mirror. Glenden looks away because he can see it in Zero's eyes too.

Then turning and turning again, and I am suddenly confused about where we are going. My current mantra is *Things will never happen to me*. I can just put them into the Yesterday Box, and they disappear like all bad things. In the Hump, I learned that fear smells like anchovies; it's impossible to miss fear when it's around. The car stops and Glenden shuts the engine off.

Sissel says, Hey Zero, you're not really going to fuck with Sheila, are you?

Zero has a small pointed nose and eyes like small black holes. From his eyes up, his head is covered by the dark brown cap he is wearing, but there is a scar from his ear to his chin on one side.

This is what I do, Zero says.

Oh, joy.

Then we are moving again, outside the car, and we stop and Zero knocks on the door. The building is not like The Home. But maybe it is.

Nothing good. Nothing good.

The girl who opens the door seems pretty at first, but when Zero whispers something to her, she looks at me and I can tell she hates me, and she looks at Zero and hates him. But she is afraid of Zero, I notice. The girl and Zero look about the same age. They don't look anything alike. Maybe different dads.

I let myself get pushed inside the apartment. It is dark and hazy with cigarette smoke or some kind of aromatic essence, but my eyes get used to it so I can see a table and a couch. Zero doesn't do anything as gracious as introduce me to his sister. Instead, he shoves the table out of the way and motions the girl to sit on the couch. I consider crushing his windpipe with a single smooth move I learned from a murderer in prison who otherwise seemed like a nice enough fellow.

But instead I let myself be pushed onto my hands and knees like a dog on the floor. Sheila is sitting on the couch. If Zero is the pornographic film-maker, then I have become the creep who says he is an actor but really is just a puppet pulled along by his dick.

I look at Sheila's face, which is bored and hating. How old is she, I wonder. Seventeen, tops? Somebody is pushing me. I smell rotten apricots.

Sissel leaves. I hear the door open and slam shut.

When it's over, I immediately try to erase what happened.

Sheila, I say to the girl, but that's all I can manage.

Zero's sister is hysterical and screams at us all to get the hell out. She's got the phone in her hand and is calling 911. Then I am being pulled back to the car that Glenden drives.

I was forced into that, I say to myself.

Before Zero gives me back my notebook, he rips out a picture of my mother that I'd colored in. His eyes have hate in them but also puzzlement. Maybe even a question. I watch him fold up the paper and put it in his pocket, then I walk away.

I try to walk back to the bus depot, but I get lost. I'm not feeling very well. My heart pounds, I begin to sweat, and my legs feel weak. So I sit down on a side street curb. I don't have any memory of this, but apparently some guy told a police officer that there was a weird person on his street and I told the police officer where I lived.

Back at The Home, the Director has called Mr. Martin to ask if I arrived at work as scheduled. When he finds out that I haven't arrived at all, I'm in trouble. Then *monsieur le directeur* calls Wendy Wentworth, and Wendy comes over just as I'm getting back from downtown in the back of a squad car. They had of course checked out my record in their data base of Everything That Ever Was, Is, Or Will Be. But I am not in violation of anything except that I should have shown up my first day of work. I don't get to shred papers that day.

Wendy is all worried about me and she asks me what happened. I tell her all about Zero, Sissel, Glenden, and Sheila. My voice is monotone.

You're pissed at me, I say.

No, Wendy says. But very disappointed. You could have avoided this.

How? I say.

You didn't have to get involved with those three particular people, she pointed out. You could have just gone to work.

And she's right. I totally fucked up.

Hank, she says. Hank, what happened to you? Is your mom talking to you again?

Then, less sympathetically: You could go back to prison for this.

I don't say anything. It wasn't my fault, I tell myself.

Did this Zero have a gun, a knife, anything that coerced you?

No, I say. He didn't.

That is my breaking point. I can't help myself and just start sobbing, like the faultless, innocent baby I never was.

Maybe what's happening in my brain is for the best. As I lose pieces of short-term memory, I think about how sad it is to have memories at all. My few remaining ones are cruelly vivid. Mom died during my first year out of prison, at a time when I was in a transition program that finally landed me here. I feel bad not being there for her. But compassion: I am incapable of that. No one living in this world has the patience to have cared for my mother. At least that's my perspective.

My room at The Home has five beds in it. It is not Paradise. That night, with the others who live in The Home in their beds after lights out, I don't worry about privacy. I see Zero's face in my head. His hatred. That I can deal with. I am thinking about Sheila, who deserves a better family, or at least a brother, one who would protect his sister from harm, from people like me.

Who am I to point fingers?

Day Whatever

More and more, once I fall asleep at night, every word, thought, or experience of the day goes into a metal box with a trap door that lets everything in, but nothing can get out.

Is that good fortune or a lousy piece of luck?

When I wake up the next morning the pictures and smell and touch from the first day are still with me. I mark the day off the calendar but I think the numbers should just disappear and be replaced with emptiness. What future is there in losing my ability to remember?

I am aware of the general order in which daily things happen. First I brush my teeth, unless I have to pee, which I usually do. So that's first. Then I brush my teeth. I get dressed by myself, come down to breakfast and have a glass of orange juice and a bowl of cereal. Then I put on a coat because if it's not cold or raining now, that could all change in a minute, a Warden tells us. We never really know what's going to happen, do we?

Then I walk to the bus stop and wait.

Another thing I can't forget, and would like to, is the day my mom was taken out of our house by EMTs, her skin luminously pale, almost white. Already underweight, she had begun fasting for Lent on Ash Wednesday and only made it halfway to Palm Sunday. She starved to death, all alone in that big house. Suicide is supposedly a mortal sin. It may have seemed to Mom like the Quik-Express line to reach Heaven ahead of the other shoppers.

Thinking those kinds of thoughts is why I am going to end up in Hell.

These episodes comprise the only memories that haven't quietly slipped into the empty box, the shadow of Yesterday. I can't lose what I did yesterday-yesterday. I try to erase it, but can't not remember.

It is not obvious, I think, that I suffer the illness that is taking me piece by piece, like someone randomly picking apples from a tree—a nice one here, another over there. Some apples fall of their own volition. *Thud*.

At The Home, a Warden makes sure we all take our pills on schedule, morning and evening. Without the support of the Director and the Wardens I wouldn't be out working on my own. They could just as well turn me loose into the World, which is the last thing I want, and is also my greatest desire.

I know how to stay alive. As if I were just another commuter, even if a frightening-looking half-child, I stand on the sidewalk with my bus pass in my right hand, waiting for the bus. I close my eyes and still see Zero's eyes, full of hatred. But something else too: fear. That makes me smile.

The bus comes to a stop but I wait until it makes a *pppfffssshhh* sound and the front of the bus kneels down, as if bowing to me.

I don't look much at the people on the bus today.

At the bus depot I see Bob, the driver who is fat and always smiling. He is between routes. I walk up to Bob and say, Hi, my name is Hank. He smiles at me and says Hi Hank, nice to meet you, and we shake hands. He is chewing gum. Wrigley's Gum Is Best by Test, I say. Bob says he's out, sorry.

I walk at a good pace to Martin and Son, for my second shot at a first day. I walk in through the front door. Both misters Martin exchange a look, then become friendly. They're being paid to give me a job by a program in the state employment security office in league with the local interfaith council social-justice committee.

Hi Hank, says Mr. Martin Junior. Good to see you feeling better. How are you today?

There are no customers in the store yet.

The Director told me I was better, so I answer fine, but I don't really remember. And I go right to work. I turn on the shredder and begin shredding one piece of paper at a time. I can't remember doing this before.

At ten o'clock I take my fifteen-minute break in the stock room in back. I am eating potato chips and a chocolate bar. I dimly consider how I will learn and then forget new things to do in the store. I entertain these gray thoughts when I hear the store's front door open and close. There are voices of men I can follow only in fragments. *Her brother ... reported ... friends gave him a ride ... sexual abuse possibly ... rape of a minor.*

And then I hear him, Zero, quite clearly saying, and I quote, The cretin raped my little sister.

Get him the hell out of here, says another voice.

I see the reflection of my face in the glass microwave door. In the reflection, I also see my mother, completely pale, distressed, as if she is trying to tell me something. I turn around but nobody is there. Wendy is right.

Although I am the size of an adolescent boy, I am a grown man with remarkable strength when I need it. People have trouble with this, with the disparity between my size and capabilities. My mother never accepted that she had given birth to me. But now that she is dead, she has become an ally, guiding me through or into the darkness. Nobody but my mother sees me take the huge, sharpened scissors from the supply closet and wrap them in paper and then packing tape. It is almost as if she is doing this through me, which of course she is, if I can believe that view.

Good, I hear my mother's voice. That's right. You'll be fine. We both know that, don't we? We never really know what's going to happen.

God knows.

I only know I'm not going back to Old MacDonald's Farm.

Mother instructs me to smite the incestuous fornicator, on this the second day. Before the Judgment when the wicked shall be left in terror and in pain on a dead and barren firmament.

I go out the back door with the scissors.

At the same time, I consider that Mom's loony voice in my head could be just me.

You and I will rise to Heaven, she says, to live in Jesus' embrace. I'm not totally convinced of that, though.

I walk back to the bus depot, finding my way easily, and stand waiting in the rain. Has it been raining for days? I feel the walls of the cell, the walls of my room, the walls around my brain growing taller.

But don't feel sorry for me. I really *am* the monster you think I am, not the nice, heartbreakingly deformed and disabled guy who lives in the neighborhood and everybody tries to be nice to. And even though I feel guilt and contrition, I'm still totally fucked.

To set the record straight, I did not mess with that little boy who the prosecutor convinced the jury I had molested. I wasn't within twenty feet of him, and there were people everywhere—parents, kids, old people, just out for a nice day in the park. He was just a kid in my neighborhood.

Now it's different. Anticipating, almost welcoming, the approaching nothingness when I can become a permanent resident of Yesterday, I wait for the low-life who thinks he has me by the balls.

I'm waiting for Zero.

The Moon Shines Tonight

In Minnesota, near the Mississippi on the Red Wing side, the sun rises out of the river, out of oak woods and field corn, now and then glancing off rattlesnake skin (as Grandma Hansen warned, cocking her head with secret knowledge of that country), below vines that hang from oak like shadows of snakes, lighting up the lattice pattern on the forest floor, rich brown, golden where the sun falls.

They moved quickly away from those woods, headed towards Knudsen's ranch to see the horses Ronnie Harlan hoped to ride that afternoon. Ronnie had seen no snakes, although he'd watched carefully, shuffling his feet through the oak leaves, avoiding stumps and rocks that might have housed a wary copperhead. Lee Hansen, his cousin who was to be married this summer—she was keeping her mother's maiden name, the name of her grandparents—didn't seem to care much about the danger. She looked often into the air, through the leaves, smiling. Ronnie tried his best to seem as if he wasn't worried much either.

With the woods behind them, Lee stepped lightly ahead of Ronnie through the crooked jogging rows of Minnesota field corn, tall as houses on either side and big around as Ronnie's arm where the stalks bore into the earth. Ronnie pushed on faster, his legs aching by now, but always he trailed a few feet behind. Every now and then he would lose sight of her and would hear only a vague rustling. As if she wasn't quite real—only a distant sound.

Ronnie thought about how things had been so much clearer from the top of Abler's Bluff, where they'd stopped on their way from his grandparents' house, just before dropping into the wooded lowland. From the bluff he'd be able to see everything: the field, the low sloping hills beyond, green-black in the early light. Knudsen's ranch. The creek flowed hidden in the trees to one side, and then, off to the west, there was the River with a cottony blanket of steam lying just off the surface, the sun rising in a red haze behind it, light clinging to the concrete cylinders of the Red Wing grain elevators that seemed to float there as well, part of the River's mist. Ronnie's grandfather, once a Mississippi boatman, used to navigate cargo barges on its waters, traveling hundreds of miles, up and down through the middle of the country. As Ronnie watched, he tried to imagine those distances. The River gleamed and twisted, pink from dawn and smooth in the morning stillness. It seemed peaceful and sluggish, like an old dog.

Back home, in the hills west of Wolf Creek, Oregon, the Rogue poured and tumbled as though it had gone insane. That was logging country. Everything was a little insane around there. Ronnie hated it.

Lee glanced from the river down to Ronnie.

"What do you think? Pretty big, isn't it?"

But it wasn't the first time Ronnie had seen the Mississippi and judged its relationship to his dreams of nearly infinite distances. Two summers ago, Ronnie and Grandpa Hansen stood, just the two of them, on the top of Abler's Bluff, a moment Ronnie still remembered clearly. The old man, sick with grain-dust disease, should have been lying in bed. No one knew he'd sneaked from his bedroom that warm afternoon when the sun glowed rust-red above the trees west of town. He'd stood there and swept his arm at the river and the wooded hills beyond, as if he were gathering something in. He told Ronnie that up in northern Minnesota there was a lake, Elk Lake, and that's where the River started. There used to be Ojibway up there, he said, and them Indians were the ones to name it. Grandpa knew all sorts of things like that, Ronnie thought.

"Yeah," Ronnie answered. "I guess it's sorta big." Lee giggled.

"You sound disappointed."

Ronnie always thought the Mississippi would be larger, much larger than the river he saw now. Grandpa Hansen had told him it was miles across down by St. Louis.

Ronnie's grandfather rested in bed most of the time these days. Ronnie knew he wouldn't live much longer, had heard his mother say as much. Anyway, that's what they kept saying, and he kept hanging on year after year like last light still suffused through the big bedroom with its carved and knobbed hardwood furniture and its flower-papered walls and lingering washed and line-dried scent of the house dresses Ronnie's grandmother wore.

Harlan Hansen was Ronnie's mother's father, a vibrant Swede. Ronnie had slightly burnished brown hair that hinted at the once flaming-red of his grandfather's, whom he resembled even in the sharp slope of his nose and in the high forehead that reddened too easily in warm weather and direct sunlight.

There was almost no way to judge their location now. Ronnie could not even tell the direction in which the woods lay. He heard Lee call, asking, almost playfully, if he was coming. He couldn't see her. Around him, drops of moisture slid like tears down the broad leaves of the corn. Then all at once, brushing through a tangle of stalks, he saw her standing, waiting. He nearly bumped her.

"Sure, I'm coming," Ronnie said.

"Tired?"

"Nah." Ronnie fought to keep from panting. It had been a long hike: from the house, Grandpa Hansen's house, out across Swede Abler's cow field for half a mile, over the barbed-wire fence and down a sandy cut bank that slid away into the woods. It was always dark in there, even on a summer day. Dark and heavy, as though the air had substance.

The creek ran through the middle, slow and quiet.

"Really," Ronnie insisted, "I'm not tired or anything." He tried to grin. He was soaked from the dew that rained on him every time he so much touched a leaf. He felt chilled and uncomfortable, but knew they must be nearly to Knudsen's ranch. Ronnie was anxious to see the horses.

Lee turned and started off once again in the lead, her long slender legs taking easy strides down the center of the furrow. Her brown khaki shorts were still creased and her light denim blouse billowed as she hiked silently along. Ronnie swept the corn aside and pushed through with his head lowered like a charging bull.

The very next thing he knew, the corn had disappeared, the sun shone, and he stood on a patch of bare, plowed ground, the field's perimeter. He gazed over toward Mrs. Knudsen's ranch: a few weathered sheds, an old stock barn, and the white ranch house settled among a clump of bright green poplars.

"Nobody's up yet," Ronnie whispered. "Let's go back." He suddenly felt foolish about being there. He worried that someone would see them standing at the edge of the field. It was as though they were spying.

"They're probably eating breakfast," Lee said.

"Let's go." Ronnie turned. "The horses are still in bed anyway."

She laughed.

"I mean..."

He guessed it had sounded a little stupid. He stuck his hands into his pockets and kicked at the dirt. The sun made his damp clothes warm but didn't really dry them.

Lee grabbed him by the shoulder.

"Look there!" She turned him in the direction of the barn. Ronnie jerked to attention and saw them: the horses. Sort of limp and easy-moving, sleepy looking, five or six of them. They drifted lazily around the corner of the old barn into the sun where the warmth made white misty vapor rise from their backs. Ronnie thought they were huge. All much too big for him except maybe the pinto that hung back in the shade of the barn and let the larger horses swish flies from its face with their long silky tails. He figured he might be able to handle the pinto.

On their way back through the cornfield, Ronnie dragged his feet in chunks of loose earth, breaking the clumps into pieces. He was tired and hungry. Once in the woods, they moved more quickly, each knowing the way through the vines and shadows of oak. Lee ran ahead of Ronnie, disappearing now and then behind a gnarled trunk. Ronnie's blood would pound, then he'd see her again, running easily. He ran. He heard her laughing, the laughter echoing through the woods and fading off.

Across the creek, its motion was a slow meandering, diverging, moving on again in a single current. So early in the morning, the creek seemed barely flowing, its surface placid. Ronnie knew its gentle contours in that stretch he'd explored with Lee on other mornings, before sun and danger of snakes made them return home. Al Dooley, the man Lee was going to marry, had come with them once. Ronnie regarded his presence as a kind of intrusion; Al had crashed through the brush while Ronnie and Lee, Lee with her private sort of grace, stepped almost noiselessly.

He heard her again, that laugh. Ronnie's side began to ache, but still he ran. He couldn't lose her. The laughter made him angry, as if she were making fun of him. He scrambled up the cut bank, grabbing handfuls of coarse weeds that pulled loose, feeling his sneakers fill with sand and rub against his ankles. She was happy like little girls are happy, Ronnie thought. As if everything were fine. He could never figure her out.

"Slowpoke!" she yelled from the rim.

Ronnie's face grew hot as he charged up the bank on all fours. The sandy slope was like a dream where you couldn't move forward.

Lee was halfway across the cow field when Ronnie reached the top. He ran, kicking dew from the grass into little flying beads that glittered in the morning sun. He saw her in the distance wiggling through the barbed wire fence, crossing the drainage ditch with a leap. Then across the graveled drive, into the front yard, Grandpa and Grandma Hansen's red frame house on Johnson Lane rising behind.

Grandpa Hansen would talk to Ronnie, and that's what Ronnie liked. Always new stories, or old ones retold with something freshly added. Never did Grandpa Hansen remind Ronnie of his father, Bob Harlan, who spoke seldom, usually to give a command. Only vaguely did Ronnie remember his father, someone standing in rubber boots under a gray sky back in the woods around Wolf Creak, thinking where the barn would go when they first bought land, judging its distance from the house, taking into account accessibility to the pasture for the stock they'd buy, wondering if the wind prevailed from the south all winter long and if cedar wouldn't be the best thing to let the driven rain pelt against the house and barn as hard as it would. Ronnie wasn't sure if he had any of his father's features; it was too long ago, even back before he could have enjoyed mulling over the coincidence (as he did now) that matched his last name with his grandfather's first, before he was aware that Harlan Hansen wouldn't be around forever, much less that his father would be snatched away by a logging accident his mother always feared was coming.

Up ahead of Ronnie, as he moved through the thick pasture grass, the house seemed warm in the morning sun, but quiet and sleepy.

"You're soaked to the skin, young man."

Ronnie's mother sat in her powder-blue bathrobe at the kitchen table. She was drinking her morning coffee and smoking a cigarette. Ronnie guessed she'd just gotten up.

"Where have you been?"

"Knudsen's."

Ronnie pulled a chair and started to sit down, hoping to be given something to eat. His stomach seemed tight with hunger.

"Not like that," his mother said. "Get yourself into some dry clothes first."

Ronnie recoiled from the chair as if it were hot to the touch. He glanced at Grandma Hansen who was hovering at the stove frying up some breakfast. She dipped pork fat from an old fruit jar and spread it in a black skillet until it was all melted. Then she cracked the eggs in. They hissed and sputtered.

"Move," Ronnie's mother said.

He went, shuffling through the living room. The clock on top of the television said seven-thirty.

Ronnie's room was just across the hall from that of his grandparents. As he pulled off his wet jeans he could hear Grandpa Hansen coughing phlegm into one of the tissues he kept in a cardboard dispenser at his bedside. It was a thick, moist sound. Ronnie hurried.

He came back into the kitchen wearing a clean print sport shirt and a pair of clean, rumpled white Levi's. The clothes rubbed a little on his damp skin. Aunt June had come in while he'd been changing, and she now sat across the table from Ronnie's mother, her hair all done up in blue plastic curlers. Lee, still dressed in her denim shirt and khaki shorts, leaned against the counter by the sink and stared out the window. "Nobody can tell you anything," Aunt June was saying to Ronnie's mother.

Ronnie crept to his chair and sat down quietly. He wondered what he'd missed between his mother and Aunt June.

"Here, drink some coffee," Grandma Hansen said, taking the blackened old Sears pot from the stove with an embroidered hot pad. She slopped steaming coffee hurriedly into the two cups, as if this would calm things.

"Drink now. It'll do you both good."

They glared at each other.

Grandma Hansen set the coffee pot back on the stove and began poking the ham slices around in the skillet.

"Your father will come around in good time," she insisted, turning the ham with a long-handled fork. "It's just his bullheadedness. You know he's always had that. Grandpa's old-fashioned in these things."

Ronnie decided they were arguing about Lee's wedding again. They went at it from the moment they got up until they went off to their separate rooms at night, usually late at night when the house had lost some of its heat and it was comfortable enough to sleep.

"Maybe we should just postpone the whole thing for another

year," Ronnie's mother said. She flicked the ashes of her cigarette nervously into the saucer of her coffee cup. Her eyes flickered briefly in Lee's direction.

"No way," June shot back. "We all know he's just doing this to be difficult."

Ronnie knew Grandpa Hansen was dead set against having Al Dooley for a grandson, but the old man would give no one any reasons.

"Well, we aren't going to fight about it now," Grandma Hansen said. "Not here in front of Lee."

The deep lines in Grandma Hansen's face pulled tighter, the way they always did when there was family trouble to be straightened out. Ronnie remembered the way she'd tried to hold things together when she and Grandpa came out to Wolf Creek about three years back. Everyone had thought the old man's lungs might clear up out West. The way it turned out, Grandpa didn't get any better and the women couldn't get along. Grandma wanted to do everything. Clean, cook, work in the garden. Drove June and Ronnie's mother both crazy.

Ronnie warmed to the plate of ham and eggs that Grandma set before him. He'd wolfed the eggs and cut into a slice of ham almost before June or his mother had lifted their forks. "We're going riding this afternoon," he said with his cheeks stuffed. The words came out garbled. Aunt June scolded him with a stern glance. "Manners," she said.

Ronnie looked at his plate. He had always felt uneasy around Aunt June, ever since she'd first come out to live with them a few years back. She'd just appeared one day with a big carload of belongings. Chairs, lamps, two heavy trunks filled with clothes and some dishes and a lot of other odds and ends. Ronnie heard June tell his mother that she'd had it with Minnesota. The folks were driving her crazy. Grandpa was impossible to get along with. Ronnie's mother couldn't say much; June was her only sister. And besides, ever since that choker cable down on the Rogue slipped and cut Ronnie's father in two, the house had seemed empty.

"I'm going to ride a pinto," Ronnie said after washing his eggs down with a swallow of cold milk. He looked to Lee for encouragement. She gazed off.

Ronnie didn't know anything about Aunt June's husband. Just

that he was Lee's father and that he was gone. Left three or so years back, right before June came out to live in Oregon. Ronnie had never seen him and Lee didn't talk about him.

"You just be careful on that horse," Ronnie's mother was telling him. He started. He'd been thinking of Grandpa Hansen. The way Ronnie used to stand over the old man's bed in the back room of the Wolf Creek house where they'd put him so he could rest. The sun would filter into the room and Ronnie would wait for Grandpa to wake up.

"Do everything Lee tells you and don't act smart or show-offish."

Ronnie felt Lee's eyes on him now.

Grandpa Hansen's presence had been the only thing that had made the summer in Oregon halfway bearable for Ronnie. He remembered how the old man would sit propped against the carved maple headboard his mother had brought from Minnesota, and how his knobbed hands would lie piled together like so much wood on his lap as he recounted some story about moving cargo and crops up and down the Mississippi in the old days. Ronnie would stand and listen, watching the parallelograms of sun creep along the hardwood floor as the morning wore on.

Lee hadn't come out to Wolf Creek. Grandma Hansen told Ronnie she had to go to college in Minneapolis. Ronnie thought that was a little funny, going to school in the summer, but he wondered if she just wanted to be away from her grandparents for a time. Grandpa and Grandma had been the ones who had really raised her, and that was why Harlan Hansen figured he had a say in her future. Ronnie thought that sounded pretty fair.

Lee finally moved toward the table, as if she were coming from a distance.

"I'll have some breakfast now, Grams," she said quietly. "I'm starved."

Grandma Hansen tilted her face, remembering something. "Al called very early this morning," she said. "He's coming over later."

Ronnie, finishing with his breakfast, crumpled his napkin and pushed his plate away, just as his father had always done when he was ready for his cup of coffee.

Ronnie was playing a solitary game of croquet on the front lawn when Al Dooley pulled his yellow Chrysler into the Hansen's driveway. It was about three in the afternoon, so humid that the sweat rolled from Ronnie's hands down onto the wooden mallet. He pretended not to notice anyone had come. When Al got out of the car and waved, Ronnie just made as if he were lining up his next shot.

Al was small, smaller than Lee, and that alone was enough to make Ronnie wonder why she went with him. He didn't seem so great. His hair swept back from a low forehead and duck-tailed behind, the way Ronnie had seen on some of the bigger kids back in Wolf Creek. The tougher kids. Al didn't seem tough, though. Ronnie thought he was maybe a little soft, the way he was always trying to be so pleasant with everyone. Always cheerful. Always that smile.

Ronnie took an aimless stroke. The wooden ball swished through the grass and stopped five feet left of the hoop.

Al was going to teach, Ronnie knew that much. Elementary school, if he remembered right. He couldn't get rid of the feeling that every time Al told him something it was like he was being practiced on. As if he was Al's personal guinea pig. "How's it going, Ron?" Al called from the Chrysler.

Ronnie made a vague mumble and waved his mallet through the grass. The lawn was too high for croquet, he decided.

"Still not talking to me?" Al was shuffling across the yard, smiling. He picked a mallet from the cardboard box the set had come in. Ronnie wondered if he was going to have to play a game with him. That's what he didn't like about Al. Always trying to elbow himself in.

"I'll stand you," Al said.

"I don't feel much like playing anymore. Too hot." Ronnie carefully replaced his mallet in the box.

"Just one round?"

"Nah." Ronnie crimped his face and shook his head. Al never got the point. "You go ahead and play through, though, if you want. It's all set up." He gestured at the diamond-like arrangement of white wire hoops on the lawn.

Ronnie knew he should have walked away right then. He could have made Al feel ridiculous, standing alone in the middle of the yard. He knew he should have but he didn't. Couldn't figure out exactly why. It was as if he was rooted. He'd just stood watching the smile fade from Al's face, slowly, as if it were melting off. Al dropped the mallet and ball onto the grass, turned, and started for the house.

The screen door slapped shut behind him as he disappeared into the kitchen.

"Good thing we waited until late afternoon. Cooler."

That was Al. Lee sort of leaned against him while Ronnie sat alone in the back seat of the yellow Chrysler.

"Much cooler," Lee agreed.

Ronnie wedged himself against the right-hand door, the one farthest away from Al and Lee. He watched the backs of their heads. Whose idea was it for Al to come, anyway, Ronnie wondered. Probably Al's. He probably just plain invited himself.

Right before they'd left, Ronnie had been down in the basement. It was cool and dark. Voices drifted from upstairs, from up in the kitchen, where Al and the women had gathered.

"Drive carefully," he'd heard his mother say. "And watch Ronnie."

"We'll watch him," Al had said.

To reach Knudsen's by road they had to swing clear out to the old Highway 29 and head in the direction of Red Wing for a mile and a quarter before jutting sharp right on a graveled lane that doubled back in almost the same direction from which they'd come. Light sprayed through the leaves of the trees that lined the way, flickering across the windshield so that Ronnie had to squint. Al and Lee had on dark glasses. Halfway there, Ronnie unfolded himself from the corner and leaned his elbows on the top of the front seat.

"You'll make sure I get the pinto, Lee?"

Lee turned and smiled. "Sure." It bothered Ronnie that he couldn't see her eyes through the sunglasses. He wished she wouldn't wear them.

"Pintos sometimes have blue eyes," Al said "Did you know that, Ronnie?"

"Uh-uh."

"They do. Means good night vision."

Ronnie hardened. He could feel that bright instructive tone in Al's voice.

"Albinos frequently have blue eyes," Al went on. He gestured with his right hand as he spoke, holding it in front of him and turning it over and over like fish in a frying pan. "Pintos, now..." the hand fluttered, "sometimes. We call animals like that, animals who function best at night, nocturnal."

Ronnie made a bored sigh and leaned back.

Gravel skittered and a puff of dust rolled up and over the car as they stopped in front of Knudsen's ranch house. A couple of shepherd dogs barked halfheartedly from the covered porch. It wasn't half a minute before Mrs. Knudsen appeared from one of the old whitewashed sheds that dotted the place, and when Ronnie saw her he thought she was the biggest woman he'd ever seen. Not fat, but husky. Muscular. She carried two big pails of fresh eggs that were still covered with brown patches of dirt and chicken manure.

"Hey!" she called out from across the yard. "Hey, come to ride?" They got out of the car.

"Afternoon, Mrs. Knudsen," Al said. "We sure did. The three of us. Mrs. Knudsen, this is Ron Harlan."

Ronnie hesitated a moment and then extended his hand. Mrs. Knudsen set her eggs to the side, took the hand and shook it firmly. Her palms were rough and calloused.

"Mind if I look around a little, Mrs. Knudsen?" Ronnie asked. He wondered if she'd seen them earlier, out by the cornfield as they'd watched the horses edge around the side of the barn.

"You go right ahead. Feel free to explore some."

Ronnie put his hands into his pockets and shuffled over to the paddock where the horses were milling. He saw that the pinto had once again situated himself so that the tails of the other horses brushed flies from his face. Pretty smart, Ronnie thought. He liked the old horse.

Ronnie climbed the wooden fence and perched himself on the top rail. He steadied himself by hooking the toes of his sneakers under the rail just beneath the one on which he sat. Below him, so close that he could have leaped right onto their backs, the horses slurped water and gnawed at their hay as if they didn't have a care in the world.

"The pinto's name is Ted," Mrs. Knudsen said. She'd come up behind him. Ronnie looked around, but he couldn't see Al or Lee anywhere.

"Ted," he repeated thoughtfully, as if feeling the word in his mouth.

Mrs. Knudsen climbed onto the fence and sat alongside Ronnie. A sprig of golden straw stuck from between her teeth.

"Shall I call you Ronnie or just plain Ron? Some boys have a preference in that sort of thing."

Ronnie thought for a moment. The kids in Wolf Creek, when Ronnie was still new to that country, used to call him by his last name. They drew out the first syllable and screwed up their mouths when they wanted to be mean or sarcastic. Ronnie almost grew used to it. To him the name Harlan sounded like age should sound; it reminded him of a smoke-filled room lined with books. He could feel wise with this grandfather's name.

"Just plain Ron, ma'am." He decided to leave it at that.

"Good. I figured."

They sat quietly. Mrs. Knudsen mauled the straw back and forth between her lips. Finally, sweeping her hand out toward the paddock and the rich green pasture that spread beyond, she nodded.

"A good place. Thirty-five years ago nothing, just like the woods you see out there." She waved at the dark line of black oak and butternut that rose stiff and dense at the far edge of the pasture. "Mr. Knudsen and I built it with out own hands. Mr. Knudsen, now, he's dead and buried. Dead five years."

"You built this place alone?" Ronnie gazed around him. The ranch suddenly appeared larger, more impressive.

"Just the two of us, sure."

Ronnie felt the fence wiggle. He looked down and saw two boys about his age crawling through the bottom rails into the paddock.

"Those are my crazy boys," Mrs. Knudsen laughed. The boys brushed the dust from their Levi's and stood grinning in front of Ronnie. "Sam," she said, pointing to the tallest: a skinny, sandy-haired farm boy with thin, tense arms. The smile he wore was like a slit across his jaw. "And Marv." Marv was shorter. The beginnings of a scraggly mustache darkened his upper lip.

"Hi," Ronnie said uncertainly. The boys grinned.

"Marv," Mrs. Knudsen said, "put halters on Ted, Kiowa and Iona. Sam, choose the tack. Get it ready." These commands she gave in a sharp, low voice. Ronnie was surprised at the change. As the two boys started off, he glanced sideways at Mrs. Knudsen's face.

"You'll be fine with Ted," Mrs. Knudsen said reassuringly. "Ted's real gentle. You two will get along."

They set out from the paddock around five. Still a good three or four hours of light. Ronnie sat uneasily atop Ted, thinking about how this wasn't like the harnessed ponies he'd ridden at county fairs back in Oregon. This was the real thing. Or pretty close to the real thing.

No, Ronnie knew, they never would have bought horses. Not useful, was Bob Harlan's reasoning. It was to be a cattle barn, the barn that Ronnie's father stood imagining on their newly bought land. Ronnie recollected that not far from where the barn seemed likely to go, a double-trunk fir rose, a perfectly symmetrical cone pointing into a sky splotched with some south-drifting clouds. They would want to keep that as a reminder of how unspoiled it was before there was even a house. Before there was even a road and Bob Harlan and Ronnie slept in the lower pasture inside an old trailer (even before his mother had come reluctantly from Eugene to join them) and the cows drifted in like clouds during the night and with the morning were nuzzling its sides, making the whole thing rock like a boat anchored in a choppy swell.

"Go into the woods by the lightning-scarred tamarack," Mrs. Knudsen had told them. She'd pointed to the misshapen tree that stood at the edge of the distant woods. Its crooked trunk rose just a little higher than those of the trees on either side. "Go in just to the right of that. There's a trail that follows the creek and you'll do well to stick close."

Kiowa and Iona were sleek bays, part thoroughbred, and with their long legs they moved quickly out in front of Ted. Al and Lee had to stop every few minutes so that Ronnie, bouncing along atop the old pinto, could catch up. Al kept asking Ronnie if he was okay.

"Sure I'm okay," Ronnie answered defensively.

Ted's ears sagged in the late afternoon heat, and the swarm of flies he'd brought from the ranch hovered in Ronnie's face as they clopped slowly along. He brushed at them with his free hand. He hadn't known it would be like this. Thick with flies. He could hardly breathe without swallowing one.

They'd ridden only fifty yards into the trees when Ronnie heard the gurgling of the creek somewhere off to his right. He couldn't see it, he could only hear it. Ted's ears pricked attentively.

"Easy boy," Ronnie whispered into the pinto's ears. Al and Lee rode ahead.

Then he saw it. It emerged to his right from a cover of sumac and poison oak, swirling thick over the gray sandy bottom. The water looked black. Ronnie watched it, half-mesmerized for a moment, then clucked his tongue and jabbed Ted's ribs with his heels until the old horse broke into a ragged trot. Like bouncing in a car down some abandoned logging road. Ronnie's stomach churned.

He thought about how he'd tried to like Al. Really tried. There was the time when Ronnie got to steer the Chrysler down Johnson Road all the way to Highway 29. That was in July, just after Ronnie and the two women had arrived from Oregon. June's Chevy Impala limped wearily into Red Wing late one night carrying the three of them plus a ton of luggage. It was raining. Ronnie could remember how there were millions of frogs spread on the highway. They turned into slime under the tires of the Impala. As if it was raining frogs and not water.

The next day there was a party where the engagement was announced. He met Al.

"This is Ron Harlan," Lee had said. "My only cousin." He and Al shook hands. Real polite.

That was the day he got to steer the Chrysler. Lee wanted to go for ice-cream, so she and Ronnie and Al piled into the car and started off for town. Red Wing was about a mile down old 27.

"Take over, buddy," Al said when they'd pulled out of the driveway. He smiled down at Ronnie.

Ronnie awkwardly positioned himself half on Al's knee and grabbed the wheel. It wanted to tug right, into the ditch, and Ronnie tugged back. He liked the feel. He craned his neck to see over the dash.

That's the way Al was. Friendly. Always tried to get you in on the fun. That's what Ronnie liked about him at first, but now he thought it was kind of a gimmick. Some personality trick.

He finally caught Al and Lee at a bend in the trail. They were waiting.

"You okay?" Al asked. Ronnie jerked upright in the saddle.

"Sure, I'm all right." The flies buzzed and crawled over his face.

"You look flushed."

"I'm *fine*."

So it wasn't as if he'd disliked Al from the start. Just that as the summer went along he began to feel like an intruder. They took him places, sure: camping on the river, Steamboat Days celebration over in Winona, three nice days with Al's folks up in Duluth. He was with them, but he didn't feel as if he belonged.

Ronnie squirmed in the saddle. A flash of late sun found its way through the lattice of branches and leaves, causing the inlaid metalwork on Ted's bridle to glint brightly.

"Hour and a half, maybe two hours of daylight still," Al said. "We'll go a little farther and turn back."

The two bays strode ahead. Ronnie clucked his tongue and nudged Ted into a slow walk. The pinto's feet plopped on the trail.

Lee, now, he couldn't figure her out anymore. She'd been okay until this summer. Always the same. Kind of remote and delicate with this habit of gazing off into the distance with her head cocked to one side like she was listening for some special kind of bird. Coolish, but that was okay. Ronnie was intrigued.

They followed the creek for a half-mile and then climbed a wooded rise where the brush wasn't so thick. Ronnie felt Ted's barrel heave between his thighs as the old pinto wheezed up the incline. The creek sounds faded below.

"This is about far enough," Al said when they reached the top. "How you feeling, Ron?"

"Just fine," Ronnie answered, tightlipped.

But that Lee. She'd changed somehow. An all-at-once type of thing, just this summer. He should have seen it right off: that very first day with Al and the yellow Chrysler Ronnie navigated down Johnson Road. Lee was kind of giggling the whole way, real happy-like, something Ronnie had never heard from Lee before. A strange laugh. As if things were really okay.

The horses nipped at isolated sprigs of grass that pushed up through the cover of dead oak leaves. Ted wheezed and snorted.

"We'd better get back," Al said.

He should have seen it, Ronnie thought to himself. Should have seen that Al was trying every way he could to get on friendly terms with Ronnie. Well, Ronnie didn't want to be friendly. Not with Al.

"See any snakes?" Aunt June asked Ronnie, teasing.

Ronnie sat tall between his mother and Aunt June, his chin

jutting out away from the rest of his face. One of Grandma Hansen's enormous suppers covered the table from one end to the other.

"Nah. There's no snakes down there."

"Oh, there's snakes all right," Grandma said. "You just didn't see 'em."

Ronnie stabbed a slice of beef with his fork and cut into it. It was tough, a little stringy. He chewed it thoughtfully.

"Well, then, I guess I just didn't see 'em."

Ronnie could think of nothing else to say. He salted his meat, cut another piece and put it into his mouth. As he chewed, the day started playing itself back in his mind, over again from the very beginning. The cycle of people and events came around like a slowly revolving wheel, flashing brief glimpses like so many still photographs. The ranch, the woods, creek running through. He could feel sand in his shoes. Hear Grandpa Hansen coughing in the bedroom.

All at once Ronnie remembered something strange which had happened earlier in the evening, when he and Al and Lee had been on their way back through the woods. He'd seen Grandpa Hansen. Or at least he thought it was him.

They'd been riding slowly, not talking much. Black oak spread and fused into a dark mass overhead as they moved along the trail. Whenever the cover of trees broke off to the left, Ronnie could see the top of Abler's Bluff rising. Bald and round, gray-green with the late summer grass. That gave him his bearings. The creek made thick swirling sounds somewhere off to the side, but Ronnie couldn't see it for the underbrush. He knew where it went. He'd followed it, with Lee. Sometimes it disappeared clean out of sight, underground, trying to find its way. And other times it broke up into two or three smaller streams that flowed separately for awhile, then joined up again and moved on, the pattern of intertwined shadows from the vines and leaves laid across its surface, seeming to hold it to its bed.

Ronnie remembered that as he'd been riding along, he started whistling. Same old tune Grandpa Hansen used to sing and play on his harmonica back when his lungs weren't so bad.

"Oh the moo-o-o-n shines too-night on pretty Re-ed Wing..."

It seemed like the only song the old man knew. He'd sing a verse in his scratchy voice and then he'd repeat the melody on the

Hohner, his cheeks puffing and collapsing as he blew and sucked air through the reeds.

Seemed like a long time ago. Ronnie had trouble getting the tune right when he tried to whistle it.

With his fork he mashed a lump of butter into his potato. The red juice from his cut of beef slid around the plate, under his peas, soaking up through the slice of bread.

Grandma Hansen got up from the table and began arranging Grandpa's supper tray. Harlan Hansen didn't eat much. Just a little meat, some green vegetables, a tall beaded glass of cold milk.

"Lee..." Grandma began.

Ronnie spoke up so fast he surprised even himself.

"I'll take it in."

Ronnie passed through the darkened living room, moving with slow, careful steps, watching the milk jiggle on the tray. Perhaps the old man escaped every night, he thought. He could picture him getting quietly out of bed, buttoning his old winter Mackinaw over the white cotton pajamas he practically lived in, slipping out through the door (which one? Ronnie wondered), out across the Swede's cow field just as the moon started peeking between the grain elevators down by the river. He would reach the crest of the bluff, his pajama bottoms flapping softly in the breeze around his ankles, and he would stare out toward the woods. Just stare for a while, then go back and lie down. Wait for dinner.

Ronnie paused just outside Grandpa Hansen's door. The hallway was dark except for some light filtering around the corner from the kitchen, making the hardwood floor gleam a little. The scene came back to him clearly. Al and Lee had been riding ahead a few yards, the two bays side by side, stepping almost in unison. A gap in the trees opened to his left, exposing the bluff, and that's when Ronnie thought he saw him. The old man, silhouetted up there while the purple evening sky arched west from beyond the river.

Of course it had been nearly dark and Ronnie couldn't be sure it was really him. Could have been almost anyone. But just the same he wanted to believe it was Grandpa Hansen, slipped again from his stuffy bedroom where they kept him under watch all day.

Ronnie cracked the door. He heard the old man's raw breathing, like something getting ground up into smaller and smaller pieces.

"Grandpa," Ronnie whispered.

He stood with the tray wobbling in his hands, peas rolling about on the plate, crisscrossing over the lean red slice of roast beef. Nothing moved inside the room. In his mind he caught a last glimpse of the figure on the bluff as it disappeared over the rise, shoulders hunched toward home.

He pushed the door wider, slipped inside and waited silently at the side of the bed for the old man to open his eyes.

"Harlan. Dinner."

Ronnie felt a shiver of premonition as he spoke the name, his own.

He waited. The lace drapes caught a breath of air and scraped against the window. After a few minutes Ronnie Harlan put the tray on the bed-stand and crept quietly from the room.

Like a Father

I sit beside Dad's grave for some amount of time. I can't remember how long. My father is buried here in southern California, and I think I was at the cemetery yesterday. I remember feeling the warm ocean breeze on my arms and an emptiness beyond loss, shame, or grief. I had nothing left to feel: no blame or guilt. Just the inner peace of acceptance. That was yesterday, or maybe last week.

Funny that today I don't remember how I got back home from the cemetery. I know I am at my son's house, sitting in the kitchen as the sun angles through the windows and falls at my feet. I move my hand an inch closer toward my knee; it crawls reluctantly along the top of my upper leg but stops short of its destination. I can't quite reach the sunlight that seduces me. Only the sun exists right now. As hard as I wish, I can't touch it. The sun will have to make the next move. I'm in a wheelchair. I believe this is where I live now.

Yesterday they bathed me.

My daughter-in-law, my son Aaron, and their twelve-year-old son gently cradled me in their arms and lifted me into the tub filling with warm, clean water. It had been a bad day, at the end of which I was looking up at the bathroom ceiling from the floor. I hadn't made it to the toilet in time. Lying on the cold tiles, feeling the wet warmth of my own urine, I was not afraid of my death. I realized that I had become the past. That's how it works.

Then I forgot about everything, content to let the water hold me, my family nearby, ready to wash my useless body with the soap and the tears they've gathered in their hands.

* * *

I remember Dad's legs were spindly as he sat by the pool in his back yard. They were so skinny, though the rest of him was built full and strong. Along the back of each calf were soft looking lumps of flesh, what I suppose could have been varicose veins. This seemed his only visible imperfection. Otherwise, Dad was what—in an era less averse to touting the virtues of manhood—could have been called a "real man." I still have a photo of him with his B-17 flying buddies clowning near the nose gunner's turret of their plane sometime during 1943. Dad was a bombardier. Doing his job as an American in the war against Hitler, he helped destroy the country from which his own father and mother had emigrated less than two decades before. My father never mentioned the war. In fact, we rarely talked about the things that mattered, and for the last ten years of his life we simply did not talk.

Dad died in 1985, in a Catholic hospital in Newport Beach, California. I had to extract that information from the police department coroner's office, after convincing them that I was his son. Now, in my late fifties, I feel compelled to write about memories filtered through decades of time, spanning the gap between what happened and how I perceive what happened, wondering, in fact, why some of these things occurred at all. In doing so, I am creating my own salvation, trying to disengage from regret and dishonor. I don't blame anyone else for putting me on the difficult road I've chosen, not anymore. Not even Dad. Like Hamlet, I just want my father's ghost to disappear and leave me in peace.

* * *

Pop didn't know who the hell Nietzsche was, nor Schopenhauer, nor Thomas Mann. He didn't read many books of any sort when I knew him. There was a time when these things made a difference to me, when I would literally sneer as I watched my father reading his copy of *Time* or *Fortune* while he sipped a drink. Dad worked hard for his success, and he was rewarded with a misfit son who held his very life in contempt, or so it seems now that I have a college-age son of my own, one who is far kinder than I was at his age.

I should not have been surprised when Grandma Blume told me not to attend Dad's funeral so many years ago. She and I had never been close, and Grandma was very protective of my dad, her only son. And yet it hurt. I feel his absence. For too many years I harbored a vain hope, somewhere under my disdain and confusion, that my father would realize I needed him.

Dad was always very close to his own parents, although Grandpa died when I was in high school. Grandma outlived both Dad and Grandpa, passing in her early nineties. Until then, she resided in Lakewood, California, in the house I remember from childhood as being permeated with the sweet aroma of Grandpa's cigars. Pa, as Grandma called Grandpa, having developed some kind of dementia by the time he reached his early seventies, passed away, so I was told, in his sleep. His funeral took place at the original Forest Lawn, just across the San Gabriel riverbed from us in Orange County.

It was open casket, one of those funerals that cleverly disguised the fact that somebody had actually died. I guess that's the point. Even Grandpa's demeanor, waxy-looking and filled with embalming fluid, was alien. I was disgusted by the way his face had been painted, giving him a garish look that in no way imitated life. Grandma smiled down at him as she walked past the casket, her lips drawn tight. Pop leaned over and whispered to me, "You don't have to look if you don't want to." But there was no way I was going to miss this. I was fourteen, and this was the first dead body I'd had the opportunity to inspect up close. But like my first holy communion taken two years earlier, it was a disappointingly empty experience. Still, somehow Grandpa once again looked lucid and sage, his false teeth placed neatly in his relaxed jaw. A few moments after walking past his body, I helped my father and brothers carry the casket out the door of the chapel, down the marble steps to the waiting hearse. Then a machine lowered Grandpa into the ground.

I had difficulty understanding these people, my family, and I admit that I made little effort to refine my understanding of them as a teenager. When I went to college, I began to absorb the despair of the German and other European writers whose books became my mainstay. Their existential gloom seemed to match the underlying melancholy of my life, during which I experienced guilt about, in my estimation, never being a good son. Could it have turned out differently—perhaps if I had known earlier of Dad's failing health? When he died, death moved a generation nearer. I've already spent a good part of my own life unhappily trying to fill the hole left by him. In the grip of this compulsion to reconcile with Dad, or else replace him, I struggled emotionally in my thirties. Just as Dad used to tell me, before we parted ways, that college is a great opportunity to find a good-paying career, my skepticism about his advice only intensified my sense of loneliness and abandonment.

* * *

I feel myself waxing confessional, as if all I have to do is lay bare my soul to lift the burden of past sins off my chest. And sin I did. I have grown so tired of avoiding the impact that my father's and my final parting has had on my life, of trying to alleviate the pain of a perhaps irreparable wound inflicted on the family's mortal substance.

But what did I know of life then? I was all of twenty years old, a student of German Romantic literature during those semesters actually spent in residence at the state university, a cow college in the Northwest where I'd gone with the intention of becoming a veterinarian. I felt myself quite special. I'd created my own curriculum, which involved reading such work as Johann Wolfgang von Goethe's *Sorrows of Young Werther*, parts of Immanuel Kant's *Critique of Reason*, and most of Frederich Schiller's poetry. I took the material very seriously, and spent long hours in the office of my mentor—an emeritus Doctor of Philosophy, and the Publishing Director at the university press.

Heinemann was an Oxford man, a German with a quick tongue, supple wit, the gleaming eyes of a fanatic, and the charm of a nobleman. The latter was acquired, I suspected, from years of luncheons with faculty wives during which he discussed the latest monographs published by his press and, of course, written by their husbands. He was something of a hero to me then, and when, for instance, I presented my interpretation of Goethe's concept of time in Faust—with thoughtful pauses to suggest an ongoing formulation of fresh discovery, even though I had written it all out on paper and memorized my script the night before—he nodded sagely and made me think I had either made an ass of myself or said something original. His subsequent agreement with my ideas surprised and thrilled me, elevating my self-esteem to even greater heights.

Socially (the word scarcely entered my vocabulary), I was shy, a quality I turned into a false virtue by striving, strutting like a pullet in a chicken yard, toward intellectual brilliance. Feeling especially akin to Nietzsche, I was obsessed with as well as terrified of women, and given to masturbatory fantasies that lasted through my sophomore year, when my celibacy prohibited even the touch of my own hand. I wept and howled my way through *Beyond Good and Evil*, and through the major works of Mann, Günter Grass (most notably, *The Tin Drum*), and Heinrich Bøll, which I now realize I little understood. I had no time for anything besides reading, and my social release consisted of reciting my poetry at a campus coffee house where I often spent the wee hours, sometimes watching the sun rise out of the basement window long after everyone else had gone home. I have since burned those solipsistic, amateur poems.

* * *

I cry on my son's shoulder as he gets ready to leave after Christmas vacation this year. I am now almost twenty years with Parkinson's disease, and Aaron is 22. He never had a chance to meet my Dad, his grandfather.

Recently, Aaron seems to have become the strong one between us.

"I might not see you guys for a while," he says as he is leaving. I'm not sure what that means. Aaron is going to try to make money this summer, fishing in Alaska, or fighting fires in Montana. He has one semester left in college, and has also mentioned joining the Navy.

Even though Aaron mostly tries to joke about my condition—just his way of dealing with it—he is now the one who gives reasonable advice. At the dinner table one night, when I was talking with him about remaining independent while living with Parkinson's, he said, "Dad, you are no longer independent anyway, so get used to it. You're lucky you've got Mom to help you. And you have the trike for getting around town." I told him I would consider his advice, but felt burned by the truth and frantic to think that if I gave up trying to get myself out somewhere and back, or relinquished any other capability I was seeing ebb away, it would be the end.

I remember a time when Aaron was a baby, crying incessantly in my arms, and I had no patience. I understand now that child abuse is a short step from impatience to inflicting pain on the helpless. Parents do not bring children into their lives with the intent of abusing. I never abused our son, but I understand the impulse. It's not just something that occurs in the moment; it's an expression of exhaustion, anger, and self-loathing that has been accumulating for hours, days, or months. Even for years. Then, one day, it just happens, and it is horrible and irrevocable.

I don't think Dad ever physically punished me or my brothers. We rarely saw him during the week, because he was always at work. In fact, my brother William told me that Mom waited to see how long it would take us to ask about Dad's absence after he moved out, and William said it was ten days before he realized Dad was gone. William may have been lying. He was hurt too.

"I think you're right about independence," I said to Aaron the next morning, when we had a stilted conversation about the previous evening. I stood in the doorway to his bedroom. He paused as if to consider whether a light, dismissive response was appropriate. Then he simply said, "Thanks, Dad."

* * *

At college, I was obsessed with the idea of escaping. That I had never been happy in the present moment may help explain why, for years afterwards, I had dreams of college, of returning there like a ghost who can't bear to leave life to the living, who feels he has yet some unfinished business in the realm of warm, sentient beings. It was my father's wish that I should choose a career and use college to prepare for it. Instead, I squandered the opportunity and equated my failure to finish college with my failure to live up to Dad's expectations.

Perhaps if I had remained imprisoned there for the full four years, such haunting as I experienced could have been avoided. But I did leave. In a sense, I left nothing behind, having amassed nothing. I had no close friends, with the exception of a married couple I'd met who would occasionally invite me out to their house in the country and worry like fussy parents that I was not eating enough. Which was true. My health, I thought, was fairly good, but I recognize now that I had a serious, undiagnosed eating disorder. I lost forty pounds in one school year. Mom was shocked when she saw me that summer. I disregarded her concern, saying only that I hadn't been very hungry. "For nine months you weren't very hungry?" she asked. I didn't have an answer, but I think it had to do with self-hatred, which had always been a component of my melancholic soul. As a toddler and little boy I was Mom's "good son." This meant to me that I was less difficult and disruptive than my older brothers. It was an early sign of the loneliness and maladaptive behavior I would come to suffer and rely on as an adult.

I spent hours at a time walking back roads, across fields tilled and frozen into hard winter furrows, along creek beds and up hills from where I could gaze back toward town and see the tower of the drama department building rising head and shoulders above the library where I worked for a few hours a week, typing Dewey decimal numbers onto book spine labels. Although I became entrenched in literature after giving up my horse-doctor dream, I still yearned for the reality of nature and often found it difficult to return from these walks in the country.

My entire two-and-a-half-year stay at the university was marked by fervid, empty aspiration. I became knowledgeable about much, but not of myself. How could I? I lived in an off-campus house as the sole boarder, a Kafka-esque shadow gazing from a dormer window, sleepless, bedraggled, utterly enchanted with what I took to be my own brilliance. My landlady was a woman in her late sixties who convinced me to come downstairs to dinner once a year, just before Christmas vacation. She was a widow; across the hall from my upstairs room was the study of her late husband, one of the school's premier chemical engineering professors.

In my dreams I always return to school to make good my ruined life, and I end up getting my old room back in Mrs. Friedlander's house. It is the only vacancy in town, and in my dream it is my everlasting punishment that I must stay there and cook my own meals on a two-burner hot plate, or else walk down the street to the supermarket restaurant where I spent my dwindling fortune on breaded veal cutlets, hamburgers, and pathetic salads laced with gummy strands of Velveeta cheese.

* * *

While in college, I still received a small but significant stipend each month from Dad as part of the child-support arrangement with my mother. The arrangement was that I would receive the money as long as I stayed in school. It paid my rent in Mrs. Friedlander's house, but there were definitely strings attached. I thought that Dad's financial support was always based on the assumption that he would get his money's worth. My unrelenting cynicism now seems at best misguided, even cruel. Each semester, I threatened to quit school, in part to spite him. But when the moment of truth came and the new term was about to begin, I was like a baseball player whose blood rises with the clarion call of spring training. Each new term found me anxious to take some new 400-level course that would, I hoped, leave me fulfilled and happy in newfound wisdom.

Just before I left school for good, I took a writing course. The teacher, who often read my stories to the class, at the end of the term remarked on the violence in my writing. "Where does all that come from?" he asked. It was just a question. He didn't mean it as a criticism, but I took it as such. When I returned to my room that evening, I pulled out a couple of long stories I'd written, including one titled, simply, "Rickenbacker," in which the decorated flying ace comes into a boy's life when he discovers that his great-uncle once flew with Eddie Rickenbacker. My story depicted gratuitously gory battle carnage, which of course I simply fabricated. I knew that my great-uncle Ressler also had other flying jobs. He flew contraband, including weapons, from Texas to various Latin American insurgent groups, or perhaps to corrupt dictators, in the fifties. I admired the romantic heroism, and saw parts of my dad in the two larger-than-life men.

I had to agree about the violence my teacher had identified in my writing at the time. I sat down to write a less sensational character study of my father, but I realized that the character was someone I was simply making up, someone about whom I knew nothing.

I'm still agonizing over how to make my father sound "real," but the truth is elusive. I realize that my image of him as sad and old arises out of my own penchant for melancholy. Acting at times like a spurned lover, I furiously blamed him for everything that was wrong in my life—my own confused and incomplete sense of family, of manhood—while at other times I wept forgiveness and wished more than anything that I could simply walk into his house, embrace him, and be his son again.

* * *

I think Aaron loves us, his parents, but he will only say it out loud when he's leaving.

He called the other night from Seattle, where we'd dropped him off on our way to Portland to visit old friends, to tell us that his Amtrak train to Whitefish had been canceled because of avalanches in the Cascades. We were more than an hour south of Tacoma. I am characteristically uneasy when he experiences a glitch and I have no power to fix the problem. But I felt only a thick inertia and apathy.

On his own, Aaron found some friends to come and get him, and he later caught a Greyhound leaving that night. How the bus did what a train could not is something I'll never know. But he arrived safely in Missoula thirteen hours later.

He's become a fly fisherman. He has fished the serpentine rivers of my memory and imagination, places in the back country of western Montana that Dad knew from the days when he and a friend were driving cross-country to take military basic training at Fort

Lewis, Washington. The Bitterroot Valley, the Clark Fork, and the south fork of the Flathead River stand out the most clearly. He went back there one summer years later, taking William, Curtis, and me fishing. Dad didn't really teach us much about fishing, just kind of let us go figure it out. We got some help from the wrangler, who suggested different lures and showed us good locations on the river.

Aaron has fished that country, too. He knows the fishing map of the Bitterroot drainage better than some of the locals. He even showed us one of his secret glory holes when we visited one year—from a fisherman, a gesture of trust and pride.

Those trips with Dad when I was a kid were good times. Most of the good times took place after he and Mom divorced when I was six years old. I keep coming back to this disjunctive episode, when the family was cleaved as with a dull, jagged knife. Mom was by no means an innocent victim in the process of divorcing Dad. My older brothers told me years later, when I could understand such things, that both Mom and Dad had been having affairs—Mom, with the choir director at our Lutheran church, a place where Dad was rarely seen; Dad, with a woman named Maggie.

***

Because Dad left the family when I was so young, I think that he never really got a sense of my introverted nature, or knew essentially who I was. I can't remember even one scene of life at home when Dad was there. By the time I was in my teens, I had spent more time with him on weekends following the divorce than I had spent with him in the first six years of my life, when he lived with us. He got to be the weekend parent, indulging his three sons with such shenanigans as miniature golf, target shooting with real guns, movies, time at the beach, and eating greasy hamburgers and french fries.

When Pop told me and my two older brothers that he was going to remarry, I felt hurt and rejected. I was thirteen. The four of us—Dad, my brothers William and Curtis, and I—were standing out in the yard on a cloudy afternoon following a day of our usual weekend activities. The weekend arrangement, I imagine, was provided for in the divorce settlement. On that day, I remember him prefacing his marriage announcement with, "Oh, by the way…" in a tone of voice he might have used to say, "Oh, by the way, did you remember to brush your teeth?" I had no idea then what the delivery of those tidings must have cost him as a parent; I certainly didn't respond with any warmth, and my brothers only asked when the wedding would be. "Well," Pop said, "We're not really going to have a wedding; we'll just sign some papers." Even then I was horrified of sex, and horrified at the idea of my father living with a woman I scarcely knew. I wondered how he could do this to us. Did Mom know?

I felt threatened and alone. The intensity of those feelings did not abate easily, and held their ground through the autumn and into the holiday season. For Christmas that year, Pop and his new wife, Maggie, gave me a new bicycle. I pretended not to notice what a lavish gift this was. They had an aluminum Christmas tree set up in their apartment, a symbol of fakery and emptiness onto which I fastened my hatred and displeasure at being there. My cynicism was extremely well developed for a thirteen-year-old. I still could not get used to the idea of my father being married to anyone besides my mother, even though Maggie seemed to like us boys well enough and obviously cared a great deal for Pop. He looked happy that Christmas Eve.

* * *

My dad's brother-in-law, my uncle Larry, had Parkinson's disease in the early 1960s. In my last memory of him, Uncle Larry was being pushed in a wheelchair outside Dad and Maggie's house. His body didn't move, and his face had become a waxy, expressionless mask. That was before the use of L-dopa for treating Parkinson's symptoms. Uncle Larry's face that day reminded me of my dead grandfather's sallow, lifeless skin.

Even with new, better medications, Parkinson's disease still takes hold and slowly destroys or impairs talents and capabilities the person with the disease used to take for granted. I am sure my having this illness has affected my son's perception of me as a father and as a man.

When Aaron was eleven, he was tall, just beginning to fill out and get strong, but he still had juvenile tantrums. He once kicked a hole in his bedroom door, and at another time cracked our car's windshield by throwing a baseball at it point blank. He had some of my wild brother Curt's dark, steaming anger. Mom said that Aaron reminded her of Curt in many ways.

But when our son became aggressive toward us during his spells, I finally had to tell him, after the intensity had lowered, that if he hurt his mom physically, he couldn't live with us. I meant it, but it hurt me to say it then as it hurts to recall it now. We were able to find a combination of medication and talk therapy that helped him turn the corner. Aaron went to counseling for a couple of years, and kept up with his meds until he went away to college, at which point he decided he didn't want to be "sedated" any more. I'm not sure what he meant; it was an SSRI antidepressant he was taking, at a very low dose, but I think there was some sense that he was somehow not quite independent or authentic when on medication. It was the first emergence of his Montana hunter and gatherer persona, an independent civilization-eschewing posture that he has apparently embraced.

Aaron's uncle Curtis has turned inward as an adult, with depression just a mishap or disappointment away. He moved to Mexico because he was so disappointed and angry with the United States and didn't want to be part of this country of war-mongers any longer. Aaron shows no signs of that kind of alienation. But his recent episode of driving home after drinking all night made my wife and me wonder about his high-risk behavior, and whether it related back to his anger as a young boy.

He is our only child, and I would do anything for him. But maybe that is not the best help I can offer. Perhaps the best thing my wife and I can do is step back and watch him fly.

I can see a time when I will need help, too. Long-term care insurance is not available to people who are actually sick, and who wants to end up in a nursing home anyway? So I make a point of not going there in my mind. For years I have been in a state of denial about end-stage Parkinson's (even writing those words causes anxiety and dread), or about disease progression at all. In my case, denial works. Without it, without the ability to selectively cross out certain outcomes, there would be nothing left to hope for.

* * *

Dad and Maggie eventually moved into a nice neighborhood in Orange County, where I visited them after I'd been at college for a year. There was a swimming pool in the back yard, and orange trees surrounded by well-kept shrubs. Avocados grew thick on a tree that shaded the pool, and on hot afternoons the coolness was welcome. We would sit around the pool sipping freshly squeezed orange juice, not saying much to one another. Without realizing it, I had already left Dad, and much of the rest of the world, behind me, growing quiet and morose as I reached the end of my teens. Maggie, who turned out to be not so bad, tactfully suggested that perhaps I should see a psychiatrist and that she and Dad would happily pay the bill. She undoubtedly saw symptoms of depression that were invisible to me. But I was proud—as though by pride alone I could maintain my sanity.

Dad went heavy on the vodka in his orange juice. I watched him drink and wished that I were not there. For five days we swam, ate, played cards, and went to the beach. Maggie tried to keep Dad and me busy with yard work. We pulled weeds and made a compost pile, but all this male-bonding activity was to no avail; in another year we would enact our last, unpleasant interaction, the result of youth's stupidity as well as what I saw as the intransigence of Dad's middle-class middle-age.

When the end came, it was as undramatic as most of life. I had received fifty dollars from Grandma Blume for my birthday, and I immediately wrote back to thank her. In a moment of insensitivity and not-so-subtle manipulation, I "jokingly" wrote that if she found any more money lying around, I could use it. Grandma was concerned that I needed money and asked Dad what to do. This was like a full frontal assault on Dad's pride and manhood as well as his financial vitality. And, I thought, it made him look bad in his mother's eyes. While I was still in college, Dad only sent me money that he was required by law to send, never an extra five or ten bucks.

He wrote a letter accusing me of preying on a helpless old woman, and threatened to cut off my funds unless I decided on a major and chose an ensuing career immediately. I took immediate action all right, and chose to destroy my future. While that impulse had little to do with how I would actually lead my adult life, at the time I was thinking mainly in black and white. Dropping out of school both thrilled and frightened me, because I saw it as an irrevocable decision.

I also did it to hurt Pop, by throwing away my own chances for what he would call success. I felt it was my only weapon against him. I've come to understand my mistake, but I remain unable to find redemption in any meaningful way. Or unwilling to, in any case. Isn't realization of and suffering for one's sins the same as repentance? Doesn't pain balance the ledger sufficiently?

There was anger in my separation from Dad, and I fired it in his direction. Before responding to him, however, I actually departed from my academic life on a midwinter flight to Mexico, a dreadful departure for the unknown. I flew to Mexico City, then traveled on to Oaxaca by bus. One day, a group of French students on the bus kept taking snapshots out the windows, at one juncture climbing eagerly out into the pouring rain to photograph a man's dead body left alongside the road after a car wreck on a twisty mountain road. They chattered unintelligibly, faces bright, as though they had just seen a good Chabrol movie in Paris.

In Oaxaca I spent the next several weeks reading Nietzsche, Peter Handke, and B. Traven, and climbing to the ruins of Monte Alban. I knew, weeping in the shadow of a pyramid, that my life was changed, horribly, irreparably, and that I had descended to a level of awareness that all was futility. No longer could I even read books, which was really all I knew how to do, so I wrote letters to everyone—desperate letters avowing and begging friendship and love. My few friends, the recipients of those letters, must have thought me mad.

To my father I wrote a message arising from my constricting self-hatred, in which I told him that I would never be like him, that I had quit school and would not return, that he could keep his money, and that I had no intention of being even modestly successful by his standards. I reasoned that I could learn just as much on my own, out in what I called the real world. As I dropped the letter into the airmail slot in the post office just off Oaxaca's acacia-shaded main square, I wondered if I would ever see him again.

Upon returning from Mexico after several months, I began having grave misgivings about the letter to my father, which I now simply think of as The Letter. I wondered what Dad, in response to The Letter, would say to me in return, and I am still wondering in the throes of my own midlife angst and compromised health. I settled in Seattle, beginning an unremarkable period of holding casual jobs, having short-lived and badly resolved affairs, writing sporadically and with some success—of Mexico, my only foreign port of call, and of the eastern edge of Minnesota where I had spent summers as a small boy with my mother's family. I applied to reenter school but never did. It was during this period that I received rumors via the family grapevine that Maggie had been abusing alcohol under Dad's nose. A few years later I heard from Dad's sister that Dad had lost his job as an executive with Lockheed. I assumed the reports true. And I partly blamed myself. I thought, irrationally, that if only I'd done what Dad wanted, what he dreamed for me, we'd still have occasion to sit poolside in the back yard while the oranges ripened, enjoying the stillness of a perfect southern California twilight.

There were times when I was content to swim alone in my dad's pool, then sit under one of his orange trees with my copy of Tolstoy, come to dinner when called, and later on play cards—canasta, if Grandma was present. That game was the vehicle by which my grandmother exhibited her otherwise hidden competitive spirit, taking pleasure in destroying her opponents as if she were a well-oiled (with quinine and lemon) German war machine goose-stepping over hapless defenders. After the game, she would invariably shake her head and claim, "If Pa vur here, he vould haff beat us all!"

But even with the occasional pleasant moment, I always had the feeling that I somehow wanted to punish Dad for marrying Maggie, and for not being the kind of father I imagined other children enjoyed and relied on.

Only now am I beginning to realize that by resurrecting an image of Dad, I'm trying to rescue myself from the oblivion I'm headed toward. At the same time, I am trying to let him go. After my first marriage ended, my longing for permanence with a woman was heightened by my abject fear of the void, of eventually losing my mind and sinking into benign madness like Grandpa, before having yet lived.

My first marriage, to the hippie daughter of a New York marketing executive, was over when I stopped paying attention to her and someone else started. The lingering memory of Mom and Dad's divorce when I was a boy, coupled with my untreated depression as an adult, made the dissolution of my marriage almost unbearably painful.

I have created and adopted surrogate guardians in place of Dad: Heinemann, the publisher who in his kindness and wisdom really was like a father to me; my high-school basketball coach; and my mother's second husband, who really raised me, even though I never quite accepted him as part of the family. I have written stories populated by central male characters. Recently, going back over manuscripts, a few of which have found homes in small literary journals, I discovered that my recurring theme was the wisdom and pain of age within older men, who feel they have lost something essential, and who yet rail against the cosmic injustice of their loss as if they could revive some misplaced or abandoned part of themselves.

My youthful rebelliousness has come full circle since I ran away to Mexico. For ten years after I sent The Letter, the fear of being rejected, and of causing even more pain for both Dad and me, kept me from seeking to reestablish contact with him. Ironically enough, his death left me wanting to be more like him, or at least like this image of him that I've since created—a good man, a solid citizen, a loving if misunderstood parent. There was comfort in attempting to live out these values, to be someone he might care to know, even though my whole life until his death was devoted to scorning his view of the world. When I was in college, I failed to realize that what I loved most in life was an illusion, and that such a life, if I had been able to create it, was not free of the consequences with which I would later become familiar. I was not aware that mortality was anything more than a literary concept. I could not envision the panic I would one day feel, reaching for the phone with tears in my eyes, only to curse my weakness as I cradled the receiver before I could dial my father's number. Or my wrenching reaction to the Father's Day newspaper story about a woman my age, estranged from her father for years, who finally wrote him a letter of reconciliation. They were reunited, and just in time—he died soon after. I read this column again and again, with a desperate fervor, as though someone had put the story there just for me.

I wasn't as fortunate as that woman. In the end, it was my Dad's heart, rather than his legs, which could no longer support him. Only after his final heart attack did I learn from Grandma Blume of his two coronary bypass operations in the years following our separation. "Did you know that your dad has been so sick?" my grandmother wrote, in a hand that had become thick and almost unreadable. I don't think she was trying to be cruel, or to blame me. But I think she was as confused and angry as I about what had happened to our family. I was more ashamed of my own feelings—that I had been cheated of an opportunity both to make amends with my father as well as to cause him more pain.

* * *

During Aaron's Christmas visit, I told him this story about my history with Dad, and the shame I carried, as we sat in the kitchen one morning with cups of strong coffee. I wasn't sure it was the right thing to do, but I reasoned that since he is the same age as I was when I began to lose my father, telling the story now made sense.

When I finished my story, cold black sludge was all that remained in both of our cups. There was a pause.

Then Aaron said, "But Dad, you're all down on yourself because you never had a chance to get back together with him, you never had a chance to please him, or anything. But what about him? Did he ever make any attempt to find you again?"

Since leaving Dad, and during the past twenty-five years, therapy and anti-depressants have helped me by easing the guilt and self-loathing, which have given way to a love for my family and my own life as a father. It hasn't been an easy or particularly heroic or even altogether successful attempt to consciously choose my road in life.

And I don't think Aaron knew what door he had opened with his observation. I had never even thought about Dad not trying to find me during those last ten years of his life. I had considered only my guilt. I had never grieved over his tacit abandonment of me, but rather focused only the flip side: my rejection of Dad and all that he stood for.

* * *

I wrote a letter to Heinemann a few months after Dad was gone, enclosing a few of my poems. I was surprised to receive a response; he complimented my work, and told me how academia was crumbling around him. He still had a copy of the paper I'd written on moral instinct in Schopenhauer's *On the Freedom of the Will*, parts of which he still maintained were publishable. The praise gave me a good feeling, until I realized that I was still seeking the kind of acceptance I have always needed so badly from my surrogate fathers, of whom Heinemann seems in my memory the most substantial and caring. In his letter he addressed me, as he always had, as "Mr. Blume." I felt as though I was still sitting on the other side of his desk, believing that such professional formality lent a certain validity to our search for meaning among the great writers of German literature. To Heinemann I was probably still the wide-eyed young man who listened raptly to his account of a meeting with Thomas Mann in Switzerland just before Mann died. In reading Heinemann's letter, perhaps it was the sense of being transported back in time to my desperate years as a student that caused me to cry uncontrollably, months after the fact, over the death of my father.

To this day, I wonder whether he didn't care what I became, so long as I set my mind to it and went after it. Maybe Dad's vision was broader than I had believed, although for a long time I doubted whether this was the case. My aspirations had always been vague and tragically romantic. Once, when I had gone home from college on Christmas vacation to visit my mother and stepfather, I announced to them that I wanted to be a philosopher, like Schopenhauer, and write fiction on the side. In fact, I did write a short story during that stay, which still remains in my cardboard box full of old writings—why, I don't know, in light of how I've burned many more "important" reminders of my past, including poems written by my ex-wife, who maintained what I felt was a tacit disapproval of my ruined, yet, she believed, salvageable relationship with my dad.

I remember clearly the writing of that story. I sat on the bed in the guestroom of Mom's house, portable typewriter propped in front of me. Sipping coffee, I wrote about a wild colt, a young cynical boy, and a weak (so I thought) yet loving father. The boy makes fun of the scruffy animal—a gift from his father—and exhibits monstrous, vindictive behavior toward the one person in the world who would do anything to please him. The father's gray, beard-stubbled face is sad and filled with incomprehension. I still feel pangs of guilt when I look at that story because it was obviously—though at the time not obvious to me—an attempt to cast him as the lost soul. But as I wrote it, glancing up from the typewriter to watch the sun flood the yard outside, a kind of caffeine-assisted euphoria and fear welled up inside me that I have since known to be associated with writing.

It was with that short story, I suppose, that I began the task of looking for my father. I've become neither much of a philosopher nor a writer, as I so confidently predicted I would during that Christmas vacation. But when Dad died, these failed attempts to find a path, any path, seemed not so much goals, as I then conceived them, as excuses to avoid living. In spite of all that I made him suffer, I have become the father that, perhaps, Dad once believed I might become. It is the same hope that Grandpa Blume, a quiet immigrant who spent his working years operating a trolley car in Minneapolis, surely had for his son.

Aaron will graduate from college and go on to build a life. That is my greatest hope. What I have to offer him now is little more than what I've gleaned from my relationship with Dad and from my failures and successes as I have tried to figure it out in a way that illuminates who I am, who we are.

The ghost of my father is fading, and yet I'm not sure I am ready to let him go.

* * *

I had a vision, a revelation really, when I lived in Seattle, after returning to the Pacific Northwest from Mexico. I was looking for a job. Having no car and not much money, I frequently took the city bus on my job-hunting trips. I was at the bus stop at the north end of the Aurora bridge, which at the time was a favorite launching point for suicides. As I waited my turn to board the bus, I saw all the adults—those already on board, and those in line— suddenly appear as the children they once had been. They were wearing tee-shirts and jeans and carrying colorful backpacks rather than the trappings of their adult lives, suits and ties and briefcases. I was envisioning their individual childhoods.

It was clear to me then, so simple but so fundamental. We all come from mothers and fathers, who came from their parents, and all the parents back to the appearance of *homo sapiens* on Earth. I felt the huge darkness inside me lighten, giving a glimmer of clarity and compassion.

I haven't been back to Mexico since then. My brother Curtis is still an expatriate living next to Lake Chapala, on whose shores, in cantinas and bullrings, the charros still rule with their drunken honor, machismo, costume regalia, and gorgeous horses. But that is another story.

* * *

Nowadays, I get around town pretty well on my recumbent trike. It has an electric motor attached, so when my legs fatigue I have some power I can rely on. I picked a three-wheeler because my balance is shot.

It's mid-January, and the park I ride through is lit by heavenly sunbeams. Every ride now is a challenge to my body. The disease fights relentlessly against my efforts. Still, I peddle down to the creek trail, where, because of recent heavy rains, the water has swollen into a white torrent, a counterpoint to the perfectly still, cold air.

As I ride into the afternoon light, a sort of mantra forms in my mind: "Yesterday's gone. Today I choose kindness and compassion."

It's impossible for me to get lost in this forested park because I know the trails so well. Eventually, they all lead me home.

* * *

"It's time now, Dad," says a familiar voice behind me. Aaron.

I want to ask him if this is Forest Lawn, where my dad was buried. The trees seem so big, like they've been growing here for hundreds of years.

My son turns my wheelchair away from Dad's grave and in the direction of the car. I'm not certain exactly the year this takes place, but it is a nice day with a warm ocean breeze blowing gently across my arms. My son sometimes tells me that I am still thirty-nine, but he knows I don't believe him. He waits until we reach the car and he's transferred me to the bucket seat from my wheelchair before he says anything.

He folds the wheelchair and puts it in the back of the car, then gets behind the wheel. He faces me, and for perhaps the first time ever he asks, "Dad, how are you doing?"

I hear him clearly, and he sounds so kind and concerned, but why now? I don't think I'm a better parent than my dad was to me. I feel like a ghost, seeing things as they really are. Like a family gathered for a photograph, my life sits in front of me, but I can't really take that picture. In the moment is where we exist, and the moment is dying.

Because Parkinson's has taken my voice, the only reply I can manage is a whisper, and I don't think he hears what I am trying to tell him.

Pure Bob

The obituary that follows is the unedited version submitted to the Wenatchee Daily World *on March 19 , 2011, by Puck Steele, the deceased's brother. — Ed.*

Bob Steele passed away, riotously, with a whoop and a holler and a "Yippee-Eye-Oh-Kie-aye," on March 18, 2011, surrounded by family, close friends, and members of Bob's cowboy poet support group, which made for quite a crowd in that small bedroom, especially with the dogs on the bed. Bob surely owed those ol' poet boys a big debt of gratitude for being there when he needed them, especially a few years back, during his recovery from addiction to alcohol in 2005 that ended a dark period in Bob's life. And they're here now, as Bob goes to meet his Maker. Born at Boise State Hospital, as was most of us kids, on May 23, 1956, Bob got into a world of trouble in the early days of his schooling. He was the oldest of us, but bee-jee-zuz he set a poor example. It's a shame he died young, but that was pure Bob. Always had to be first, or best, preferably both. Bob left home when he was 15. He headed west to Wenatchee, Washington, and picked Washington Red Delicious Apples grown along the Columbia River. He liked the Mexicans he worked with and I guess they showed him every courtesy in return. After signing up for the Military when he was 18, he served with the 4683d Air Base Group at the Thule Air Base in Pituffik, Greenland, as a Mechanic. Bob liked hunting and cheating at poker, two of his favorite pastimes. He lived in Missoula, Montana, for many years, and learned to ride a horse and herd cattle in the Bitterroot Valley. Bob Steele is survived by his parents, Mr. and Mrs. Edward "Duke" Steele of Boise, Idaho; a brother, Jonah "Puck" Steele, also of Boise; and sister Margaret June Steiner of New York City. He is also survived by an Aunt, Edith Cather, *nee* Steele, and his favorite hunting dogs Socks and Killer, as well as nieces and nephews who were not allowed to play any card games with Uncle Bob when they were younger. Sadly, Bob was preceded in death by wife Carla Jo Steele and daughter Elizabeth Solace Steele, both tragically killed in a car accident in 2002. That was the start of Bob's darkest hour, and you can thank any of these here cowboy poet fellas for getting a purchase on Bob's soul when it needed lifting up. Once Bob discovered cowboy poetry and took a stab at it himself, he couldn't stop writing. Bob climbed onto that horse, he stuck his butt to the saddle and kept on keeping on. He left notebooks full of random lines and jingles, and published 3 books of poetry before his death. He knew nothing would bring back his wife and daughter, and he always said that if he could stop writing poetry, he probably should. Writing was so hard that it was killing him, or so he believed. Well, it succeeded in doing just that. Bob has stopped writing. But we can still hear his voice, ringing lonely and clear out with the sagebrush. Bob wanted to be cremated, so we're going to have a remembrance of that son of a gun at Veterans Memorial Park here in Boise, on Saturday, April 1 (April Fool's Day; I think Bob would of gotten a kick out of that, if he was around). No flowers, no booze. Just bring some Perrier and a covered hot dish to share. If you want to honor Bob's memory with a gift, send a donation to the Dead Cowboy Poets Society. But mostly we would be awfully pleased if you just showed up. I don't know anything about my brother if I don't know he'd love a crowd of people who were still alive enjoying an afternoon telling their own "Bob stories," laughing and crying, all of them stone sober. Come help us give the old boy a whoop and a holler that they'll hear all the way over in Horse Heaven Hills!

silent pictures

... exactly twelve. At first there were an even dozen lined up in two rows of six on the top shelf. Their authenticity: unquestionable. The light flick of a fingernail was the acid test. Crystal.

Bavarians, my father's parents had little knowledge of or interest in the *Shoah*. They assumed *Reichskristallnacht* must have been precipitated by the Jews.

A scene follows. It is set in a Minnesota farmhouse in 1948. The main characters are a one-eyed Siamese cat and a ruddy-cheeked woman in her sixties. The cat is sitting on its haunches, not on the floor, but about five feet above the floor, on top of a cabinet where the fine crystal-ware of the house is apparently kept. The cabinet is of dark hardwood, gaudily carved in a rococo fashion. They had brought it over from Germany in the late 1930s. One of the glass paneled doors to the cabinet is swinging open and inside, the crystal goblets on the top shelf are tottering on their stems like drunken flamingoes. The cat seems to be waiting to see if any more of them are going to fall out onto the floor. The ruddy-cheeked woman stands with her hands on her hips and is about to say something like: "If you weren't blind in one eye, Missy, you'd be in a lot of trouble!"

... tirelessly retrieving empty pop bottles from the Mississippi River during a hot Minnesota summer. Line them up on the grass and throw rocks, connecting on about one out of ten. The sun glints on the sharp fragments and you wonder if cows can eat broken glass and live.

In America, they refused to believe what people were saying about *Dachau*, *Sachsenhausen*, or *Buchenwald*. They were happy being Germans.

Grandma sometimes let me take Grandpa down to go swimming in the afternoon. We'd swim and then loll about in a mud-bank until we were black. That was Grandpa's favorite time to tell me stories about his life in the German Cinema, and if I didn't stop him the mud would dry on his skin and crack so that he'd look like prehistoric mud flats.

In Minnesota I was never bored. I had the river to play with. It was a muddy river and full to bursting with enormous catfish. So much junk in that river you wouldn't believe it. A million empty pop bottles.

A young whey-faced man wearing a starchy collar is sitting in a folding canvas chair. A director's chair? It could be my grandfather for all I know. It is the first photo in the album. Turn the pages and see, at the end, an old whey-faced man wearing a rhinestone collar while standing on all fours. He's imitating either a German Shepherd or an undersized horse, and a very small boy, all smiles, is sitting majestically on his back looking into the camera. "Hey! It's me!" his smiles seem to say. It could be me for all I know. Click. Minnesota, 1948.

My grandmother kept her crystal goblets in a rococo cabinet by the kitchen thermostat. The cabinet was guarded day and night by a Hoover upright vacuum cleaner and a brown garbage pail.

Grandfather made motion pictures in the silent era. He met D. W. Griffith in England in 1932. In the latter part of the 1930s, encouraged by Griffith, he decided to come to America to direct films in Hollywood. He and Grandma came to America but never made it to Hollywood. I can tell you something about his German movies. They were failures, every one of them.

Grandpa and Grandma moved to Minnesota where they bought a farm. There, something went wrong with Grandpa and he spent the rest of his life parading around as a German police dog.

One of his movies required a one-eyed Siamese cat. That's how he met Grandma. She had the cat.

Not the same one that watched the shattered goblets in 1948. That was a different one-eyed Siamese cat. The motion-picture cat never left Germany alive. The Minnesota cat outlived my grandfather. In dog age, Grandpa was 445 years old when he died.

Two plates of food sit waiting in the kitchen of a Minnesota farmhouse. Potatoes, cabbage, gray hunks of boiled beef. The little boy gazes skeptically at the cabbage. On his right sits a crystal goblet filled with fresh milk. The rococo cabinet is standing behind the boy with one of its doors open and because of the gaps on the top shelf appears to have been mildly raped.

Grandma made casseroles in the silent era.

Cabbage, milk, goblet. The boy takes a large swallow of milk, hoping that maybe the cabbage will disappear. An old ruddy-cheeked woman in her sixties is silently eating the meal.

… the boy, thinking, "I want to take Grandpa down to the river," but Grandpa doesn't seem to be around. A one-eyed Siamese cat perched atop the violated cabinet is peering either at the milk in the goblet or at the goblet surrounding the milk.

There was a crowd scene in Spain. One thousand Roman Catholic extras had to march past the camera on their way to Mass. "Don't look into the camera," Grandpa had the interpreter emphasize.

That was Grandpa's most elaborate failure. He had plenty of them right there in Germany which weren't elaborate at all.

He didn't mind talking about Germany. "Life in the cinema was… fascinating. Aside from the expected ups and downs it was … totally rewarding. My leading ladies were always quite… exquisite."

… thinking you're Huck Finn or somebody but later finding out you're not. Empty pop bottles from the river get broken under a summer sky and mirror a fragmented portion of the family portrait. Your dog runs away and you spend the next year and a half combing the woods for telltale signs of an animal on the move.

On his four hundred and thirtieth birthday I bought him a cheap rhinestone collar and sat on his back while Grandma snapped a picture.

There is a cabinet with a one-eyed Siamese cat on top. A ruddy-cheeked woman is eating her meal. Potatoes, cabbage, boiled meat. Everything in a boy's life is safely guarded by a Hoover upright vacuum cleaner and a brown garbage pail.

A falling crystal goblet in 1948 somehow prophesied Grandpa's death. Not exactly clear how the goblet was dislodged. Only the one-eyed Siamese cat knows for sure. Actually, the cat had two eyes but only one worked. The one that didn't work looked like a glass marble.

Another huge swallow of milk empties the goblet. Does the boy dash it to the floor?

… where, as before, cabbage sat rotting. Finally, the little boy dashes it to the floor. He will not eat cabbage.

Empty pop bottles rise from the depths of the river and bob to the surface like pale, bloated corpses. Grandma lets me go down to the Mississippi as often as I want to collect bodies. Cows, I discovered, can eat broken glass and live.

    Grandpa could not survive the advent of talkies. Silence was always his genre, and it had served him well as a good German and a patriotic American.

Scene. A crystal goblet has just left the shelf of a rococo hardwood cabinet and seems determined to hit the floor. A ruddy-cheeked woman cannot stop it even with her bulging eyes. Two miles to the left, a mud-bank on the Mississippi plays host to a boy and his wildly gesticulating companion. Mud flies. "Life in the cinema…. My leading ladies…." Mud.

    Safely atop the cabinet, the cat turns a blind eye toward the woman. A glass eye like a marble, unbroken.

    The goblet is going to hit the floor. The upright Hoover has failed. The brown garbage bucket—failed. Nothing it can do but collect the pieces. "If you weren't blind in one eye, Missy!"

A young whey-faced man used to make German movies in the silent era. He needed a one-eyed Siamese cat and found Grandma.

    Grandma was the only one to see the goblet fall. The only one, that is, except for the cat. The Minnesota cat, not the other one. Grandfather and I were off imitating mud.

    The river ingested bottles and later regurgitated them. It was like a biological function. Grandfather and I could not know that the goblet had fallen when it did. We should have guessed; like all rivers, the Mississippi was a depository for junk, the more so because of its size. So much mud in that river. A million bottles.

The goblet eventually reached the hardwood floor. "If you weren't blind!"

The cat turned an eye. He never did own up to clairvoyance.

Despite efforts, the cabbage would not disappear. The boy held a secret desire to adorn himself with the muck of a riverbank. Grandpa did not seem to be around. Something had gone wrong with Grandpa and he decided to become a German police dog. This was in the forties after the war. The safest place for a one-eyed Siamese cat was atop a rococo cabinet.

Behind me, above an open door, a cat was perched, and although my back was turned toward him I'm sure he was staring at my goblet of milk. So I drank the milk. I'm sure he was staring at the goblet as well. An old ruddy-cheeked woman sat across the table silently eating. She too had been a good German. How anyone can eat cooked cabbage I will never understand. Although my back was turned, I could picture the open-doored cabinet where the goblet originated, the two interrupted lines of crystal vessels tottering, the path of the now-perched cat springing.

And the boy enamored of mud. Stranded bottles stuck their hollow necks up through the black Mississippi sludge before being sucked away. In the pasture old glass caught sunlight, cows ate the grass and lived.

But even with the advent of talkies, Grandpa stuck to silence.

The End of the World, As Witnessed by David Pickles

1.

Charlie Partum was, by most accounts, even his wife's, an average and not completely fulfilled man. Moderate ambition had placed him in a comfortable station in life. After studying political science in college, he set off into the world and 45 years passed, at the beginning of which he'd fallen into a business career that had nothing to do with politics or science. Finding that he was good with numbers, he got a job as an accountant, eventually starting his own business. Near retirement, Charlie wondered about the future, what to do, and why. Directions for changing his life and re-inventing who he saw in the mirror every morning had not been included.

Years before, Charlie and his wife Jocelyn were among the first to buy a new house in the suburban housing tract that included the Dandelion neighborhood, a parcel of once-forested land due east of the skyscrapers and urban life encircled by the interstate highway. It had been Charlie's idea to settle in the Dandelion neighborhood. He liked the idea of living outside the city.

Thus they migrated out beyond the encircling Beltway, an eight-lane merry-go-round of traffic, leaving urban life behind to the younger, more desperate, and better-armed generation of technology and financial wizards, who seemed only too eager to work themselves into death or a long-term care facility, for which they wisely obtained insurance early in the game. Charlie telecommuted two days a week so had to drive into the city only three. He grew tired of working.

The Partums had always wanted to live by the water, with a nice view. And so, when Charlie Partum fully retired, he and Jocelyn sold their three-bedroom rambler on Dandelion Street and bought a cottage on Lake Ossett (people in the county pronounced it OH-sit), which was actually a reservoir of opaque brown water held in place by a dam that featured spillways and tunnels, a road across the top bridging the two shores of the lake, and advanced flood-control engineering, as well as a fish ladder, should any fish actually exist in these waters.

From Dandelion Street to the Partum's cottage on Lake Ossett was actually not that far. The first time they went to look for their dream piece of heaven, they simply turned right on Division Avenue in their late-model Nissan Altima, which was a quiet, smooth ride, and drove along the river for a couple miles until Division became Newport Boulevard. The same road eventually veered right toward Newport, a mid-sized town with a hospital and a handful of buildings rising to a by-city-ordinance limit of ten floors. But no port, to speak of.

The Partums took the smaller street, Lakehurst Way, that tracked due west to where Division turns into Newport. They drove Lakehurst another mile uphill, past a few mail boxes, and finally arrived at Highwater Place, which dead-ended, actually becoming a cul-de-sac, with access to three houses set twenty yards apart on the shores of Lake Ossett. Theirs was the one in the middle—a cottage, Jocelyn called it. That's the one she knew from the first moment was going to become their place, their new home.

The houses on either side were summer rentals, so the Partums worried about feeling isolated in the winter months. But they moved in, kept an eye on the lake, built fires in the woodstove in the winter, found the isolation refreshing, and before they had realized it, three years had passed.

2.

Although he had lived a relatively contented if not extremely happy life, Charlie Partum said one day to his bride of 42 years, as they sat looking out the window of their lakeside cottage at the ripples on the lake, "Joss, memory is so sad. Do you feel it? We have memories and grown children. Where the hell are they? And photographs."

Jocelyn Partum's face shriveled in concern. Her husband wasn't a depressed or gloomy man, but a quiet one who thought things out for himself before opening his mouth to speak.

She answered with a thoughtful-sounding *"mm-mmm."* She and Charlie had been going through boxes of old family photos, trying to organize them, but it seemed a fool's errand. Charlie gazed into each photo with such intense concentration that it appeared to Jocelyn that he went *into* that photograph with people whose names neither of them could remember.

Charlie's wife worried when he continued gazing into a faded black and white snapshot of Charlie as a boy standing with his dad in front of an elevation sign at the top of a mountain pass: "4,856 ft." the sign read.

"Is this somebody we know? They look familiar. Oh, maybe not," Charlie said, handing the photo to his wife.

3.

Just as the Partums were deeply involved in trying to understand Charlie's mental fibrillations, a younger man, David Pickles, was about to have an experience that would both terrify and excite him.

David had been half-dozing in his Newport home, shared with his wife Jenny and his daughter Miska, on a cold day in April. He had turned up the gas fireplace thermostat to 75 degrees and was looking through Dr. Sevren Vandeuver's recent book on optimizing management of medications for Parkinson's disease. David's neurologist had suggested he read it. Desperate to learn about what he had been fighting in the dark, without a diagnosis, for more than five years, David Pickles until recently hadn't known its name.

"If we all lived until we were ninety or even a hundred," Vandeuver wrote in his Introduction, "we would all develop some degree of parkinsonism. When new dopamine cells start to die off or not be synthesized at all, we are left only with the picture of a patient's caregiver filling from a hose the leaking bucket the patient is holding. After time the leak grows larger and the dopamine precursor, levadopa (the water from the hose), can no longer be added at a rate and strength that will completely control symptoms without causing even more disabling side effects, both physical and cognitive."

David took his Parkinson's medications, Sinemet and ropinerole, at the times of day his neurologist had indicated to the pharmacist, who in turn typed on the pill bottle label that same information. When David started on the ropinerole, the neurologist carefully titrated the dose up to 6 milligrams per day, and then said they would watch his reactions for a few weeks.

Steve Benson, the pharmacist, whose mother had just died last week, and who was working both the hopper and cash register because his assistant had no-showed, handed David a prescription medicine bottle filled with three-milligram instead of the prescribed one-milligram tablets. Generic ropinerole tablets of different potencies all looked the same except for the color. David needed the green tablets, not the purple ones, but he checked the dose on the label and it confirmed one-milligram.

Benson asked David if he had taken the medication before.

"Just what's in the free titration packets I got from my neurologist," David told him, not sure if it was okay to divulge the fact that he got freebies.

"Any questions?"

David said no as he swiped his VISA card, took the bag containing the bottle of pills, and signed the receipt, carrying away a 3-month supply of tablets.

"If you experience alarming side effects," Benson said, "Please either call us or contact your doctor."

David said fine, while wondering what side effects could be alarming. He was about to find out. For thus did David Pickles start, unknowingly, taking 18, not 6, milligrams of a very touchy brain drug every 24 hours.

At home a few days later, quick glimpses of dark creatures seen out of the corners of his eyes made David believe he was seeing things. When he turned to look, though, there was nothing to see but the things he was familiar with: the dining room table, the huge HDTV flat screen, the original paintings by a well-known regional artist whose work sold for up to $5,000 per canvas. Then, David saw what *had not* been there the last time he looked up. A woman with dark brown hair, not as striking as his part-Cherokee wife Jenny, but attractive in a way that had always been invisible to David in women that he ignored or took for granted at the office. She was just there. Then she turned around and walked back into the kitchen and was gone without a sound.

She reminded David of the Cylon beauty referred to only as Number Six in *Battlestar Galactica* who controls by her sheer sensuality, not to mention super-human strength, the hapless Dr. Gaius Baltar. Only Dr. Baltar is able to see her.

Although David had never seen this woman in his life, he intuitively knew her name: Sarah, with an *H*.

David had diagnosed himself with Parkinson's disease at age

47, thanks largely to the Internet, which had made his amateur diagnostician's task exciting, until he determined what he had to deal with. When he told Jenny, she thought he was being a hypochondriac about some vague symptoms. She had been trying to get him on antidepressants. At age 48, he received a Parkinson's diagnosis from a neurologist in Newport, the once-small town in which he had grown up. But Jenny still didn't believe it.

Newport actually had an identifiable downtown, and many of the businesses in town when he was a kid were still there, passed down by parents or grandparents. Clark's Feed & Seed was still across from the ice cream shop. It was as if no one had told the business owners that they were no longer relevant. David's opinion was that they were more relevant than commuter traffic and condos in the air, but he could see both sides, because he'd been one of the desperate, younger, better armed telecom commandos, and had also moved and repackaged mutual funds as a money doctor. By the time David was forty, the terms *derivatives* and *toxic assets* were part of the language of financial markets, and David was neck deep in the crap.

As a boy, David had a very nice singing voice and seemed neither more nor less inclined to become an important, wealthy man. At age ten, he wanted only to learn to play the guitar so he could be a rock musician and scream blistering vocals like Kurt Cobain. His parents told him he would have to make enough money himself to buy a guitar. That delayed the lure of rock stardom.

Offered parts in various school productions such as *Les Miz* and *Little Shop of Horrors*, he always turned them down, because he was busy coming up with all manner of moneymaking schemes. Most of these were innocent as a lemonade stand. For a while, he stood on the corner waving an advertising board for a pizza place. He really wanted a metal detector, but he stuck to his original goal of buying a good guitar. The biggest mistake he made was asking Grandma Pickles for a sizable contribution, for which she would become a silent partner in the band, as if the nonexistent group was already on its second sold-out platinum tour. His dad made him give back the money to Grandma, and issued a warning.

The other reason David Pickles chose not to participate in school performance events was simply that his last name completely embarrassed him and was already the punch line of too many jokes.

The guitar was forgotten after a few months, but David had learned something about venture capital: never solicit startup money from your grandparents.

4.

A box of David's old family photographs was out on the coffee table in his living room. Some of them 80 years old, the black and white snapshots revealed a world that had literally disappeared. One picture, of David and his Grandpa Hansen, his mom's father, standing in grandpa's back yard, with nothing beyond them but open fields, spoke to a time when a town like Newport was more like a living organism with a central core than an endless, redundant grid of streets, lanes, places, courts, boulevards, avenues, and parkways running in all directions of the compass. Grandpa had a brother who owned a farm outside of St. Claire City; a photo of the stacks of hay in his field brought back vivid sense memories.

The photo project would take a while, David realized. His wife Jenny wasn't as interested in the past.

Just the week before David met Charlie Partum, Jenny and their daughter Miska were off to visit her parents, who lived in a gated community called Walnut Creek Estates, just a quarter-turn counterclockwise around the beltway. Jenny wanted to give David some space, and was also tired of his obsession with this illness of his. How long would that last, she'd wondered.

Miska didn't like Walnut Creek, because it was like no one really lived there. She never saw anyone, let alone children, outside the houses that were painted different colors but all looked the same, with big garage doors and easy-care, unimaginative landscaping.

David and Charlie, of course, didn't know that they were going to meet. But as these things sometimes go, it was fated to happen.

5.

Speaking with David, Jenny referred bitterly to Parkinson's as "your" disease, and she wanted no part of it. Hurt and feeling abandoned, David couldn't fault her reaction. Her attitude wasn't unreasonable. There they were, living a normal American life, raising a daughter, financially secure and socially connected, and then this *monster* appears, threatening to take that all away. David's was a relatively young age to experience loss of dopamine-dependent neurological function, and it was indeed surprising to him to learn that by the time symptoms showed up, four years ago, his brain had already lost eighty percent of its dopamine-producing capacity. David knew those things because he had studied the disease, while Jenny expressed her fear indirectly, showing impatience with his obsessing, still believing it was something her husband was making up. If he wasn't making it up, what would their lives become?

The best David could suggest was that they get away, maybe rent a house on Lake Ossett for the summer. He thought Jenny would protest because of money, but she embraced the idea without hesitation. David could drive as easily to work from the lake as from Newport, she suggested to her husband.

They were able to get through the whole next week without saying anything about Parkinson's disease. David even kept quiet about his trips to see a neurologist inside the Beltway, and to the pharmacy at FoodBuys in Newport.

David called a guy he knew who owned a property management company in Newport and found what looked like the perfect place, out a couple miles on Lakehurst, on Highwater Place. Bob Tyler warned David that it was not fancy and might be too rustic for his family. The place usually rented out to *working people*, retirees, and younger people low on the ladder to success who couldn't afford more upscale lodgings. On the plus side, there were large cottonwood, maple, and oak trees among which all the houses on their side of the lake nestled, and it was right on the water. It sounded just right to David.

The retired couple who lived in the next house over was *very* nice, Bob said. They were owners. On the other side of the Partums was a young couple in their twenties who lit a Fourth of July fireworks display that rivaled that of any city neighborhood.

In fact, Charlie Partum thought they must have spent a fortune. But he and Joss sat on their lake-facing front porch and watched the searing explosions high overhead, the smoldering remains floating down to fizzle in the darkness and despair of the lake, simply ceasing to be.

As the Partums often did when summer renters arrived, Charlie and his wife invited their temporary new neighbors over for cookies and coffee. It had been beer and nachos with the young couple. The Pickleses arrived on an overcast June day in the afternoon, driving an immaculate new red Honda Element.

"You have to give them a day to settle in," Charlie said to Jocelyn, who was peeking through the bedroom blinds at their new neighbors.

The next morning the invitation was proffered and accepted, and the coffee and cookies served.

6.

Charlie noticed the trouble the young man, David Pickles, was having with his lower body. David froze in the doorway and couldn't move his feet. He put his hands on either side of the doorframe, took a deep breath, then concentrated not on taking a step, but on lifting his knee. From the physical therapist he had leaned this trick: he had to take his attention away from his feet and put it elsewhere. Then he was able to walk. Doorways were the most difficult.

"Hello, Mr. and Mrs. Patton," Jenny said brightly. "It was so nice of you to invite us over."

"You're welcome, dear," said Jocelyn. "Just so you know, however, it's Partum. Like in post-partum, after you have your baby."

"I'm so sorry," Jenny apologized, "Mrs. Partum."

"Nothing to worry about, Jenny. And please, just call me Jocelyn. Charles calls me Joss, but that sounds too much like a cowboy. Remember Hoss, on *Bonanza*? Big, sweet man." Jocelyn surprised even herself with her excitement, just talking to someone other than her husband.

Jenny, of course, being of another television generation, had no idea what show Mrs. Partum was talking about. *Bonanza*?

Jocelyn tuned to face David, took his hand and said, "Is it Parkinson's, dear?"

"Well," David Pickles said slowly, clearly embarrassed, "I've been diagnosed with … with ah … a neurological disease. Actually, yes, it is Parkinson's."

"We're not positive!" Jenny almost screamed, then explained. "David is something of a hypochondriac."

David, at that moment, wished for nothing more than to have Sarah appear and replace his wife. Face flushing, he said nothing.

Miska Pickles-Phelps, six years old, was tired of listening to this adult conversation. Having none of her father's lassitude, Miska was bright and aware of how lucky she was to be six years old. Inside her there burned a bright flame that she rarely revealed. She asked her mom if she could go outside and play.

Though she was still upset, Jenny smiled and said, "Just stay where we can see you."

"Okay."

"Would you like to take a cookie out with you?" Jocelyn asked.

"Yes, please," replied Miska.

Outside, it looked to Miska like there were no other kids around. In fact, she didn't see anyone else around. The place was so quiet, just the gentle lapping of waves on the shore of Lake Ossett. Across the lake, there were clumps of houses, set among the trees, modestly sized residences just like over on this side. As a small boat putt-putted up the lake, Miska saw the man sitting backwards in the boat holding a fishing rod.

Her dad owned a fishing rod. All Miska could figure out about her dad now was that he'd changed. Which frightened her. Like when she had walked toward her parents' bedroom Sunday morning, bringing the newspaper so they could all read their favorite parts, she heard her dad talking to someone, not Mom, because she could hear her mom out in the kitchen rattling pots and pans and creating wonderful smells of things baking and frying.

Miska hurried into the kitchen. What she had experienced was scary, and she asked her mom who Daddy was talking to.

"What do you mean," Jenny asked. "When?"

"Just now, in the bedroom."

Jenny panicked, then pulled herself together in order to walk back to their bedroom. Miska stayed in the kitchen.

"David," she said. "David, what's going on in there?" She walked in and saw her husband, David Pickles, lying on his back in their bed, moaning. "David!" she said. He was slow to startle. She said his name again, louder, "David! What are you doing?"

Her husband looked up at her blankly. "What?" he asked, dazed. He couldn't remember where he was.

7.

David Pickles wondered if he should seek psychiatric help. But he *knew* what was wrong. He had figured out that he was overdosing on ropinerole. And he could control it, at least to some extent, for now. Yet he experienced other hallucinations—such as seeing the starting line-up of a pro baseball team, including last year's Cy Young award winner Carlos Fuenia entering his bedroom one night late after Jenny had gone to sleep, looking at him, and filing back out, all in silence.

It was a secret, David Pickles thought, a secret so revealing and powerful that he feared for his sanity, and indeed for his life if he let it be known to his family, or for that matter, to anyone. But he wanted to keep it. He wanted desperately to *keep* it, without asking himself just what would happen if he kept *it*. No one, he thought firmly, no one would understand me having an affair with a hallucination named Sarah, who only he could see.

He remembered the ghost on the TV show "Topper," broadcast in the early '50s, in which the actor Leo G. Carroll played Cosmo Topper, who with his wife Henrietta moved into a house haunted by its previous owners. Or was it the other way around? David thought that only Cosmo could see the ghosts, who seem likable enough, with middle class attitudes, a sit-com sense of humor, and neat, pressed 1950s clothing, including ties for the men.

David and Jenny tried a support group for people with Parkinson's disease and their *caregivers*, a new term for Jenny that scared the hell out of her. She was 36 years old, and taking care of anyone other than her daughter was not on her list. David asked the group moderator about hallucinations—were they a result of the disease, or was it a side effect of the meds? He didn't mention Sarah.

"Is anyone else experiencing hallucinations?" asked the moderator, a young neuro-psychologist just out of Emory. "By which I mean day- or night-time episodes of seeing something or someone who is not really there?"

No hands went up.

"Well, briefly, it's an issue with the disease process, which includes a medication regimen with a dopageneric therapy aspect that can certainly impact visual as well as aural perceptions. Some patients have these false perceptions, others never do."

Back at the house on Lake Ossett later, when Jenny and Miska were playing checkers at the kitchen table, David, in the living room, opened his Vandeuver book on Parkinson's.

Vandeuver wrote: "The causes of Parkinsonism can be determined for some manifestations of the disorder. An example is stroke-induced vascular Parkinsonism, which resembles idiopathic Parkinson's disease, but is in fact caused by a series of micro-strokes that result in symptoms, including large motor skill deterioration as well as worsening dementia, probably with Lewy-body involvement, that characterize PD but do not respond to levodopa therapy or other symptom-ameliorating pharmaceutical interventions."

David was laying the book down on the coffee table in the living room when he felt a sweet-and-sour taste develop in his mouth just before Sarah appeared, walking into his field of view from the corners of his eyes, then standing immediately in front of him.

8.

Charlie Partum was lying in bed one morning at the lake, in June of their third year at Lake Ossett, and the drift of his musings went something along these lines:

How much we think we know about death, examining it from every conceivable perspective, except for the one that would show us the real story, after we die. Meanwhile, in life, we flounder without a clue as to what really matters, and we squander our souls on meaningless amusements, and around and around the world goes.

The Pickles clan, as he privately referred to them with Jocelyn, were a sad story. Heck of a burden to have that disease so young.

But Charlie Partum wasn't doing too well either. He knew that something was up. Having trouble with his memory was nothing new, but it seemed worse now. Charlie could easily become disoriented, especially at night. With malaise a dark current pulling him down, the lake water took on a new, menacing aspect.

"Joss," Charlie said one day, "I want to move back home."

"Sweetie, this is our home now. Did you forget?"

"I think I want to move home to Dandelion Street. Where we usually live."

"Used to live, darling," Jocelyn said patiently. "Used to live."

"Well, I don't like it here now."

Jocelyn felt bad about Jenny Phelps's situation. They hardly talked, the two women, but that was because neither of them had any idea of the other's desperation and need.

The boy from next door, Brady—that's how he had introduced himself the week before—walked over to the cottage. Banging on the front door, he yelled, "Hey, Mr. and Mrs. Partum, radio says there's a big storm system that's going to blast right through here! So batten down the hatches! Due tomorrow early morning. Just wanted to let you know!" Brady and his girlfriend left Highwater Place, and maybe the state, that night, after boarding up the shutters and locking the door. The cable TV lines didn't run this far out yet, so news was more or less word of mouth. When Charlie tried to use the radio, all he could get was static and one Hispanic-speaking AM station.

Then, the strangest thing: Charlie noticed that David and Jenny's car was also gone, as the sky was darkening, but there were still lights on in their house.

9.

"The real sign that you are going crazy and losing your mind," David Pickles wrote on the back blank page of his Vandeuver, "is that you aren't *aware* that you are going crazy. But how is it possible to be aware of not being aware of your mental condition? You need an observer completely outside your own perception to assess your actual condition."

Jenny said she couldn't handle being here any longer. With David. She was taking Miska and they were going to stay for a while in Walnut Creek Estates with her parents. Just like that, they were gone.

He had the book marked to a section he had just finished reading. As the darkness outside began to rustle with summer cottonwood leaves stirring in a light breeze, David read another section of Vandeuver's chapter on hallucination and delusional thinking.

"Those patients on a regimen of dopageneric medications, primarily a combination of levedopa and carbidopa, as well as one of the dopamine agonists, such as ropinerole, if they are predisposed to delusional thinking, paranoia, visions, and having crazy ideas, may well find that hallucinations can appear even in young-onset patients, or those in the early stages of medication. My first choice for quelling or eliminating altogether the occurrence of hallucinatory episodes is Careticopine. This drug is less likely to cause worsening of Parkinson's symptoms and should be used only if withdrawal from Parkinson's medications, especially dopamine agonists, as described in the previous section, has not been effective. Any change in drug regimen must be discussed with the neurologist prior to any alterations the patient may believe reasonable."

David was exhausted, something he'd been feeling more and more. He was taking his medications on schedule and knew he was due for some soon, when he realized that he had no way to get out of here without the Subaru. Jenny had of course taken it to her parents' house in Walnut Creek Estates.

The first big gusts came through about four in the morning. Jocelyn Partum was sleeping on her side in their bed, muttering in her sleep, her mouth open, deeply unconscious. In the living room, Charlie Partum sat on the floral print sofa, gazing though the window and hearing the wind rise but unable to see anything in the pre-dawn gloom. In the next house over, David Pickles slept in his reading chair, his body stiff and uncomfortable since his bedtime dose of meds had worn off about an hour ago. His copy of Vandeuver lay on the floor next to him where it had fallen. The lamp next to the side table next to David was still on. David, in a restless sleep, wasn't aware anything had changed when the light went out. Charlie, however, sitting in the darkness waiting for dawn, felt something shift, perhaps a change in the light wind's direction. It seemed quieter. He thought the refrigerator, suddenly silent, must have been cycling through its automatic temperature adjustments.

These were the only three people left on Highwater Place, none of them realizing that two enormous air masses of conflicting temperatures were at this moment colliding over Lake Ossett. Charlie Partum heard a distant but approaching roar that came closer and suddenly exploded into the trees, the water, and the cottage.

The wind didn't last long, nor did most storms in this part of the country—they tended to blast for an hour or two, then slowly back off.

By dawn it had gone to an aching sigh, tentatively shifting its bearing from southwest to westerly. The warm June air had been cooled and now felt cold as a grave. Charlie fumbled with the door latch on the front door of the cottage, even though he could have almost walked out of the hole that, until hours ago, had been a large window.

When he was outside, nothing looked familiar. There were huge tree limbs the size of anacondas floating out in the lake. The lake's surface looked scrubbed and clean, with whitecaps still breaking in the direction of the dam.

Charlie had left his clothes on through the night. Jocelyn had been terrified, screaming above the Freightliner-truck pounding of the wind.

Things don't just happen, Charlie thought, trying to get a picture of how this event fit. Like he had said to Jocelyn last night, he wanted to go home, to Dandelion Street. Why didn't she just say, "Yes, let's go now, Charlie. You were right."

The storm confirmed for Charlie the reality of Nature's malevolence.

"Joss," Charlie said again to his wife of 45 years, "I want to go home now."

Every house on the lake had lost power and phone lines. In Charlie and Joss's cottage, there was a battery-powered lamp and the licking flames in their woodstove. One of the cottonwoods had blown over right onto the unoccupied house in which the young couple was having breakfast 24 hours ago. Thick branches stabbed through the roof like it was a pincushion.

10.

David Pickles made his way over to the Partum's cottage, dazed as he stared at the gaping hole where the lakeside picture window had shattered. "Mr. and Mrs. Partum," David called softly, fearing they were dead or in need of emergency medical care. "Charlie. Jocelyn," he called again, pushing open the door. They were sitting on the sofa and looked very old to David, but did not appear to be injured.

"I think I know what's going on here," Charlie said. "This is the end of the world. Nature is taking the earth back, and this was just a warning."

Jocelyn looked at her husband and knew she was losing him. She would be his lifeline from this point forward, as he drifted into deeper dementia every day. Although, wasn't caring for Charlie what she had been doing for the past 45 years?

"The world's not ending, dear," she said, facing her husband. "It was a terrifying storm, but it's over and we'll pick up the pieces. It'll be okay." They seemed almost not to notice David standing in the doorway. David saw that things were not going to be okay for quite a while. His family had left him, and his life seemed to be in free-fall. On the way to the bottom he was entertained by horrible grimaces of those fiends he knew so well: shame, despair, failure, regret. Near the bottom, he finally got a clear look at his own stupidity, his ridiculous secret, and the fact that he had created a world he thought was under his control.

He backed away from the Partums' front door, gently pulling it closed. It didn't seem to fit right anymore. His tremor reminded him that he had missed a dose of medications. Walking back to his empty house, he thought his mental—he couldn't really call it "health" anymore—his mental collapse could be a sign from God, as Charlie had suggested. The prophecy of Daniel came in the form of dreams, he mused. The foretelling of the Apocalypse. "I am going insane," David said aloud as he walked across the scoured rock from which the topsoil had been blown.

But, at the same time he felt that if he thought he recognized his insanity, there was still an observer in his consciousness that argued against an insane condition. Wasn't real insanity the loss of the observer, making the delusional the usual? David smiled at the rhyme, thinking he would remember it when he tried to explain everything to Jenny.

His meds were in the pill organizer near the bathroom sink. As he grabbed for them, with the beginning of a physical desperation as his brain cried out for dopamine, he saw movement on the periphery of his vision. He shuddered, then turned, expecting to face Sarah, with an H, but she was not there. Somebody, something, had taken Sarah's place. Standing before him was a hallucination in the form of David Pickles. It was not like looking into a mirror or seeing oneself in a photograph or movie. It was like looking at a ghost.

Somewhere in his mind, the thought arose: I wonder what Vandeuver would make of this. Maybe I'll write him a letter.

Neither Charlie nor Jocelyn Partum, who were staring out the space where the window had until recently been located in their cottage, heard the howl of terror that came from David Pickles's house.

They shivered in the icy wind that blew through the room, but Jocelyn Partum noticed that, for the first time since they'd moved here, the water in the lake was no longer brown, but had turned a beautiful, foam-speckled blue.